Sea Pictures

Also by Janis Spehr and published by Ginninderra Press
Leaving Ray

Janis Spehr

Sea Pictures

Sea Pictures
ISBN 978 1 76041 123 7
Copyright © Janis Spehr 2016
Cover photo: Stephen Matthews

First published 2016 by
GINNINDERRA PRESS
PO Box 3461 Port Adelaide 5015
www.ginninderrapress.com.au

Contents

for Veronica

Venice

Kate and her long-time friend Venice were walking down a street in the small seaside town where Kate now lived. It was a cold day in early spring; a leaf solitary as a tear brushed along the footpath but some of the trees were covered in shouts of blossom. The town was a tourist place. Beneath milky skeins of cirrus, people sat bravely sipping al fresco lattes at spindly aluminium tables and various shops displayed their wares on racks.

Kate kept stopping, rummaging and flicking and holding things up for Venice's appraising eyes. 'What about this? Does this look any good?' she kept asking, holding up fabrics spotted and splashed with quasi-Aboriginal designs, black velveteen retro-hippy pants, shirts on which dolphins sported or koalas lunched.

'Oh, no, no, no…no, god-awful…'

Venice wore one of her own creations, a square-necked purple tunic slashed to show an underskirt of day-glo green. On most women this would have looked ghastly but Venice managed to carry it off. 'I am my own best model,' she had proclaimed to the Centrelink assessment panel when she paraded her business plan, tricked out with Powerpoint diagrams, two years before. The panel had agreed, had given her a year's funding which had paid for an overlocker and the rent on a shopfront. Now Venice sold her clothes from the shopfront and even supplied certain outlets in the city, although she had confided to Kate the previous evening that she still didn't make enough to live on and occasionally had to do a telemarketing shift, just to make ends meet.

She had never been to this town: she had come down to hand over Phillip and to check out opportunities at one of the markets held during the summer holidays.

There were few places outside St Kilda where Venice was happy. Kate could tell that she was already bored and restless so this morning she had suggested a walk and they had ended up at this strip of overpriced consumer goods.

Kate was trying to think of an excuse to turn back. She was yearning for a sandwich and an honest cup of milky tea, when Venice threw the T-shirt at her.

'What the…' Kate held it out in front of her. A gabble of words covered the famous face but after a moment she put the features together and did a few dancing steps with the shirt. 'Oh, Che, Che, Che Guevara,' she chanted. 'Che, you tragic lefty martyr riding your motorbike through the jungles of Peru…'

'Do you want the green one or the pink one?' interrupted Venice. 'Green's better with your eyes.'

'Well, Che would have hated pink.' Kate picked up first one shirt, then the other. Che's defiant face stared out from rococo splashes of gold paint and fractured lines of print.

'Don't cross that line…you'll wind up dead…' Che had wound up dead, somewhere. Kate couldn't remember the Latin American country where he had finally been gunned down, leading his band of ragged, footsore guerrillas who must have known it was all over for their particular brand of revolution. Che, who gave up privilege to struggle for the downtrodden masses. Che, who had set up the first concentration camps in Cuba for political dissidents and homosexuals. Yes, Che would have hated pink.

'I'll take the pink.' Kate threw the shirt over her shoulder and headed to the shop door. She looked around for Phillip, who had been trailing them ever since they left home but he was already inside chatting up the sales assistant.

'Veni-son,' intoned Kate, waggling her index fingers from her forehead in threatening, pseudo-antlers. When Phillip was three this had reduced him to hysterical screeching laughter but he was sixteen now and he just looked at the girl with a long-suffering expression.

'Don't worry, he's not responsible for me. They let me out of the locked ward every Sunday.'

The girl gave Phillip a conspiratorial half-smile and folded the shirt. She had a skin like blushed cream, flawless and poreless, shiny dark hair caught back with an ornate leather clasp and many rings featuring large, semi-precious stones. Che would have liked her, Kate thought. She watched while the girl tucked in the sleeves neatly and smoothed the neck, which had been left frayed and unhemmed. The shirt had been slashed in places and the slashes repaired with wild zigzag stitching.

Kate reached out and lightly stroked one of these wounds, letting her fingers brush the shop assistant's. 'Look at this. You can turn anything into a commodity. You take a revolutionary life with a pretty face and it ends up in some free trade zone, being sweated over by someone who six months before was standing up to her knees in a paddy field. But that's history, isn't it?'

The girl gave a nervous laugh and looked at Phillip, who shrugged again and examined the ceiling.

How low have you sunk, Kate asked herself, as the girl held out the pale pink cardboard bag inscribed with the shop's name in silver, that you have to compete with your friend's son, a boy you've practically raised as your own, for female attention? Was she turning into a sad, middle-aged lech? It seemed that everywhere she went these days she was constantly distracted by the sight of spandex-covered thighs or hair like spun gold or a fetchingly tattooed navel.

'Thanks,' she mumbled to the girl.

Outside, Venice stood holding a cigarette, watching the smoke drift towards the clouds. She was still striking, with her olive skin and ravelled hair, but time and the drugs had submerged her beauty. You looked at Venice and thought of watery things a long way down or of some coin dug up after decades or even centuries, the soil clinging to archaic inscriptions and a proud profile obscured by grime.

'Walk with me.'

As soon as they fell into step, they held hands. This made Phillip look the other way then cross the road.

'What is it with these…displays of homophobia?' exclaimed Kate. 'He was never like this! Never!'

Venice shrugged. 'Perhaps it's an attempt to establish some separate masculine identity.'

'I thought that was meant to happen earlier. Anyway, he seems to be doing all right. You said he had some little girlfriend at school?'

'Yeah. Besotted.'

'He is?'

'No, her. Chloe. She rings him all the time, sends him texts and emails. He treats her badly. He often doesn't reply.'

They laughed and stopped for ice cream at the small park in the centre of the town. Kate couldn't help herself; she ducked into the public toilet and pulled the new T-shirt on underneath her light zip-up jacket then sprawled companionably with Venice, licking chocolate chip pieces in rich vanilla.

Right in front of them was an artistic achievement recently unveiled by the mayor. An androgynous figure balanced on a mess of twisted metal, one leg raised, looking as though it was trying to take flight, but forever stabilised by the ruin below.

'Just another idea that didn't make it off the ground.' Venice yawned and reclined against Kate's ribcage.

'How's the sculpture garden?'

'Rusty.'

This was how they had met, all those years ago, Kate and Venice, when Venice still referred to herself as a painter/sculptor and Kate was between jobs, fed up with the petty politics of the women's refuge and yet to start her third stint as a public service clerk. This was the eighties, when all kinds of altruistic ideas prevailed about making the unemployed self-sufficient through creativity. Many different people, film-makers, poets, dancers, multimedia artists, climbed upon the governmental gravy train. They got paid, for six or twelve months, to set up projects fostering initiative, self-awareness and, hopefully, useful skills. Kate remembered Venice, wearing only a black bra beneath faded overalls and resembling some kind of postmodern bushranger underneath her mask, her hair tied back with a printed Indian scarf, sinewy forearms gleaming as she wielded the blowtorch.

'I fell in love with your welding skills,' she told Venice, while they watched kids scream and contort on primary-coloured playground bars.

Venice snorted sleepily. 'Fat lot of good it did you.'

'Not true. I may never have become the world's greatest oxy-arc tradesperson but it did teach me something about art.'

'Not much good as a career foundation, though, was it?'

'At least I had a good time. Anyway, you don't need a foundation to do what I do.'

When Kate first arrived in the town, she had worked in the local tourist centre but it had driven her insane. She hated the horrid suffocating girliness of it: the need to control the growth and smell of her feral armpits, the manager's demand that she constantly smile at the visitors so that by the end of the day she felt as though her face was curled in a plastic surgery rictus. There was constant bickering among the staff about how the brochures should be arranged. The language: 'Shall I just pop that in a little bag for you?' 'What part of the world are you visiting us from?' And the music! Dreadful collections of whales cooing and dolphins bleating that were supposed to soothe frazzled tourists trying to choose between bed and breakfast and motel-style accommodation. Much to the manager's displeasure, Kate had resorted to bringing in her own CDs – the Stranglers, the Clash, Siouxsie and the Banshees.

Now Kate worked in one of the local servos as day manager, which was really a euphemism for general dogsbody, although she got to organise the car wash, the workshop and the lolly shop ('retail outlet'). She was responsible for the banking and the work rosters; she enjoyed the smell of the grease and the high-pressure whoosh made by the pneumatic gun for putting on tyres. The blokes who worked there were no hassle; they called her Queen Bee because of the regal way she dispensed receipts for petrol and ice cream in the lolly shop.

She glanced down to where Venice lay softly snoring, bumped her shoulder, then bumped it harder. 'Get up.'

Venice giggled dopily, yawned and stretched. 'Where's Raph... Phillip?'

'Over there. I've been keeping an eye on him.'

Phillip was slouchily in conversation with three kids on the steps at the base of the war memorial. The steps led up to a small rotunda where a hundred years ago a brass band had sweated to entertain citizens on summer afternoons. The names of the local dead of all the numerous wars in which the country had been involved were inscribed on granite plaques on the outside of the rotunda but Phillip and his new friends were oblivious to this history. The girl, who was pasty and plump, like so many girls in this town, sat on a step, looking up at Phillip and a boy who held a skateboard and had his hair done in dreads. A light bruise ridged a cheek and one set of knuckles was cross-hatched by a reddish-brown graze. An accident, wondered Kate uneasily, or something more confrontational? The other boy had chunky hips slung with a studded leather belt and a blue heeler dog on a lead.

'Hi, guys.' Venice, that matron with a perennial teenager's heart, charmed the kids, she had them eating out of her hand, the boys wanting to go to bed with her, the girl wanting to wear her dress. She knew the names of the bands to which they listened; she made a few self-deprecatory remarks about being 'just an air-headed fashion designer'.

Kate stood listening in wry amusement, Philip glowering behind her, but almost before they knew it, it was done: Venice had extricated all three and headed them towards Kate's place. Kate glanced to the top of the rotunda, where a weather-stained angel, managing to look both surly and camp, unfurled his wings and raised a chipped sword to the sky.

'And the *Ball and Chain*? That's rusty too?'

'It's in better condition than most of them.'

'Shit, we had a fight about them, didn't we?'

'Yep.'

They looked at each other and laughed. Every member of the group had been charged with the task of designing an individual sculpture, although creating each piece would be a group effort. Kate had sketched two women reclining, arms and lips locked.

'This hand's too large. Out of proportion.' Venice had taken the pencil and done some reducing work.

'She's eager, wants to have it all. To have and to hold.' Briefly, Kate's gaze rested on the breasts beneath Venice's blue op shop shirt.

Venice ignored her and went on sketching. 'Figurative sculpture's passé. Do something different. Something cutting edge, abstract.'

'Abstract's not beautiful.'

'Beauty's boring. Surprise me.'

'I'll fucking surprise you.' Kate tore the sketch in two and started again. She nearly put the pen through the paper as she drew the cone and sphere. 'There! Where I come from we'd call this *Ball and Chain*, as in *Mick left the ball and chain at home with the kids and went to the pub*. You, on the other hand,' she turned to Venice and thrust the drawing into her face, 'would no doubt call it *Wife's Lament*.'

Venice looked at her watch: gold, engraved, undeniably expensive. 'Ten past four. Do you want to go to the pub after we finish? You could leave the kids at home.'

They went to the pub. They drank a lot. Briefly, that evening, they reclined, arms and lips locked. Life imitating art, Kate thought, as she splayed Venice beneath her, her fingers wet with her, holding her wrists as she buried her mouth in the streaming dark hair. Venice had been glorious and Kate had seduced her away from that crowd of black-wearing heterosexuals who sat in bars and coffee shops, the arrogant boy painters and photographers who agreed that women could be artists but who chose as their partners attractive girls who went out to work to support them. Kate had gone out to work to support Venice for a while although it was Venice who found the scungy flat above the kosher butcher in Acland Street. On their first anniversary, she gave Kate a model of *Ball and Chain*, made by a silversmith friend of hers, which was tiny and exquisite as jewellery. She brought home some pure white powder…

Kate looked across the street, where Phillip had resumed his shadowy stroll. Up ahead was a last cluster of civic buildings – police station, Anglican church, kindergarten – before the streets gave way to agistment paddocks and the few straggling houses which lined the land above the estuary. A constable who didn't look much older than Phillip sat idling one of the cop cars in front of the police station.

'*Tenez le Droit*. I've always thought that was such an appropriate motto.' Kate stopped directly in front of the windscreen, facing the kid. She bowed deeply. With one perfect downward swoop, she unzipped her jacket and bared Che to him. She bared Che to the world. Then, giggling, she and Venice passed on, leaving the kid furrow-browed and goggle-eyed.

'You bloody ratbag. Just as well he's not a senior sergeant with a personality disorder, wanting to make life difficult.'

'Nah.' Kate picked up a stone, flicked it into the reed-filled sludge of the creek where a few ibis waded disconsolately. 'They know me. They think I'm a ratbag but harmless.'

'Oh, dear. Harmless.'

They started up the track threading the edge of the embankment. Below, the creek gave birth to a shallow fan of water. Concerned residents regularly wrote to the local paper about the green-skimmed, mosquito-ridden estuary, calling it a potential health hazard and an eyesore. Kate loved it. She supposed that sometime soon a deal would be struck between a developer and malleable members of the council. The estuary would be drained and cleared and luxury apartments built where the half-dozen ramshackle houses now stood. She would be out on her arse again, but for the time being she sat tight. Hers was the highest house on the ridge so she escaped most of the mozzies and on hot, humid evenings she opened all the windows and took a canvas chair out onto the splintery old veranda, letting John Coltrane unfold his sax behind her. Some nights she'd have a couple of joints as well as a few beers and the music would wrap around the inside of her head like sinuous gold.

She and Venice climbed past Neil and Trixie's place, then said hello to the old woman with the Rottweiler who never returned a greeting as she watered the lawn. The Murphys, that family of peripatetic dole-bludgers and fishermen, weren't home and the shack that the alcoholic plumber from Geelong used for his weekend benders was closed and dark. Misfits, thought Kate, with a small surge of pride, although the house before hers was occupied by a perfectly normal social worker and arborist. Glancing up, she saw a figure sitting on the veranda with a guitar and realised that Phillip had beaten them home.

'Go in, mate,' she called. 'It's open.'

'Oh, my,' said Venice. 'Unlocked doors. I know I'm in the country. Where are the scones, jam and cream?'

'In the fridge. The scones are a bit stale. I'll give them a zap in the microwave.'

Kate set out the stuff on the table and brewed coffee for herself. She was starving but for the time being this would have to do. She steeped a bag of green tea and took a Coke from the fridge for Phillip.

'Have you got everything from the car?' Venice took the teabag from the cup, squeezed it until it crinkled like an embryo then placed it carefully on her plate.

'Yeah.'

'You sure?'

'*Yes.*'

'You better have, because be buggered if I'll post anything for you from home.'

Phillip didn't reply. Clutching the guitar by its neck, he slammed the door and, ignoring the rickety set of steps, jumped from the veranda to the strip of couch grass in front of the house. He kept going, through the stretch of weeds which had overtaken the grass and out through the rusty front gate to the lip of the embankment.

'Watch your step, watch your step,' muttered Kate.

The embankment was prone to subsidence, particularly after rain. She and Venice lay at either end of the old sofa in the lounge, eating the zapped scones and the excellent jam from the local berry farm while Phillip squatted in the clay and gravel escarpment, his back to them.

'Do you remember the night we made him?'

'Not very well.'

The line of white powder had lengthened considerably since the night of Kate's birthday. Venice had given up sculpture and painting and started working in one of the parlours on Robe Street. For a while she had justified her behaviour by citing all the famous junkies in history: 'Look at Rimbaud, look at Burroughs, all those fifties jazz musicians like Coltrane and Bird. They were always sticking stuff up their arms or up their noses. It's just experience.'

Kate had screamed and raged as the mountain of snow grew higher. For a while, she even tried to bury herself there too but she was squeamish about blood and snorting the stuff only made her vomit. There was the wonderful parallel addiction of the bottle and so many bottles to chose from. Kate had loved the one which held a particular Eastern European brandy, the light striking diamonds from its cut-glass sides and the stopper ornate as a Byzantine mosaic. The liquor itself was colourless and tasted like petrol. That had been her favourite for a while.

Kate sipped her coffee and let the slightly burnt taste linger on her tongue as Phillip took his singlet off and threw it on the ground, where the wind caught it and spun it around like a hunched and feral animal. From where she sat, the long dragon twisting the diagonal length of his back was just an inky smudge but Kate felt the singing line of pain where the needle had bitten; she felt the tender red ridges holding a dark river of hurt.

'That tatt must have cost a fortune,' she murmured.

'We had a bit of a fight about that. I wanted something more life-affirming, a tree or something.'

'You think it was the Vietnamese guy, that night?'

'Christ, does Phillip look Vietnamese?'

'The dragon might be some sort of race memory thing.'

'It's much more likely it was the Lebanese.'

Kate recalled that it could have been one of half a dozen. Even with her scrawny junkie pallor, Venice was popular, although she claimed that looks had nothing to do with it. 'All they want is a cunt to come in,' she would say dispassionately, watching the flame lick the spoon. 'If I had a television up in the top right-hand corner of the room, my job would be so much more interesting.'

She stopped working after the first five months. Phillip was born on a cold, blowy morning in August even though all their astrological advice had predicted a girl. Kate gave up her job and looked after him while Venice went back to the parlour.

'He was a good baby.'

'You were lucky.'

'It wasn't just luck. Even the social worker said I'd done a good job.'

'Not good enough.' Venice laughed shortly.

'If she hadn't taken him away, you wouldn't have gone to detox. You wouldn't have been gloriously saved while you were there and come to Jesus. You were a real pain in the arse then, just as bad as when you were using.'

'I was not,' replied Venice serenely, draining her green tea and lighting up. Cigarettes were the only stimulant she allowed herself now. She never drank alcohol or touched tannin or caffeine. Even after her rebirth into a glittering, hard-edged warrior for Christ, she'd smoked. After she caught the pastor's eye and married him, she gave up lipstick and kohl but not nicotine.

She let the cigarette smoulder in the dolphin-shaped ashtray Elizabeth had found in one of the local op shops and reached for the last scone. Despite her disclaimers to hunger, she had eaten them all.

Kate grinned resignedly and reached for the orphaned half left on the plate. She thought longingly of Bernie Murphy's trevally fillets in the fridge. 'Do you ever see Ed these days?'

'Not for a long time. He still sends things to Phillip, for Christmas and his birthday. He used to try to inveigle me back to the fold but he stopped after a while.'

'Ed always had a certain *savoir faire*. I'm sure he never told you that you would "perish in the flames for all eternity", the way you used to go on at me.'

Venice smiled, shrugged. 'I was looking for answers. I'd nearly died a couple of times. People I knew were dead. I thought there had to be a reason for all that.'

'And now you know there's not?' Kate remembered the small room with its rows of chairs, the neat drum kit and acoustic guitars, all a backdrop for Pastor Ed, that Baptist alpha male, charismatic in every sense as he conducted his healing ministry, looming over the prostrate

Venice. Phillip had been five when he was ripped from Kate's life; for years there had been a crater there which nothing filled. When he was eleven, Venice had run off with Ed's sister-in-law although the first Kate knew about it was an email from India several months after the fact:

raphael arriving Monday a.m. at Tulla. can u collect? sending money & clothes.

Kate had been living on the east side of Melbourne, during a protracted house-sit for a pair of wealthy old closet cases who had decided that they simply must spend another summer in Italy. She battled into the city with the rest of the commuting drones then flowed on westwards to the airport. The boy already had the demeanour of someone constantly on the move. Self-contained but not passive, Kate thought as she embraced him. Clever, too.

'Mum's left you holding the baby again,' he remarked, staring through the windscreen at the traffic on Alexandra Parade.

'She'll be back soon.' In some ways, Kate hoped so. Adele and Clarissa hadn't anticipated a child running around their porcelain and antiques. Venice's second email had mentioned amoebic dysentery. 'She said she'd be back just as soon as Auntie Sylvie's better.'

'Auntie Sylvie.' His voice was putrid with venom. 'That old muff diver. That old bitch…'

Now Kate gathered up the smeared plates and sticky knives. She glanced surreptitiously at her watch: she longed for a gin and tonic. As she bent to retrieve the mugs, two tears, perfect as mercury, slid down Venice's cheeks.

'Uh, oh.' Kate leant over with an awkward, crockery-laden hug; then she put down the dishes and hugged again. She sometimes glimpsed this well in Venice, a bottomless subterranean river of grief which rarely oozed above ground.

'What if I lose him?'

'You won't lose him but you need to say goodbye to him, now.'

'Sometimes he looks at me as though he hates me!'

'He doesn't hate you but he needs to grow up a bit. Go and say goodbye.'

Venice collected the sample shirts, extravagant creations made from contrasting strips of silk and brocade, she had taken to impress the woman who allotted stall space for the market. She threw her overnight bag into the boot of the Mazda she had once described as butterfly blue but which was now fading to grub grey. She hugged Kate. 'How's the new woman?'

'Not fascinating but occasionally thrilling. I like her even though she has a hairy face.'

'I was hoping to meet her.'

'And you might have, if someone's racehorse hadn't pulled a hamstring this morning.'

'Next time, then.'

'Next time.'

Venice threaded her way through the weeds then stopped to pick out the burrs sticking to her skirt. The wind lifted the skirt to show long thighs which Kate knew were cobwebbed with dead blue veins, wrinkly as an unravelled piece of old knitting. The wind propelled Venice, looking almost skittish, still clutching her skirt, towards the boy, who spread his arms like wings. Venice bobbed her head, darting, supplicating – Kate recognised a caricature of the behaviour with the teenagers in the park— but Phillip turned himself into a dervish, his hands like fans, scissoring the air.

Venice recoiled but Kate didn't go out to her, just watched her run past the house, her face a lattice of tears.

After the sound of the Mazda faded, Kate poured herself the promised drink: teetotallers were always a pain in the arse, no matter how noble their reasons for abstention. She took out the trevally fillets, turned them briefly in a chilli marinade and put them under the griller, chopped vegies and threw them in the steamer. She made herself a second g&t then waited. Phillip appeared just as she put the food on the table.

'You want a drink?' Kate asked casually. 'There's a lemon Cruiser in the fridge.'

'Coke's fine.'

He disappeared into the small side room he'd chosen as his own. He kept the door shut. Kate imagined it as a compost of sweaty boy clothes and explosive sexual dreams. When he returned, he wore a grey T-shirt featuring an attractive, sharp-featured woman sitting by a roadside. 'Will work for sex,' read the caption.

He opened the fridge, looked at the Cruiser but didn't touch it. 'It was just a bit of under-age drinking,' one of the cops had told Venice. 'It wasn't as though he was doing anything really bad.' But there had been the stolen car which could have killed someone. Phillip wasn't the one who ran it up onto the kerb and into the lamp post. He'd been in the back seat with another kid whose arm had snapped on impact and who had suffered mild concussion. Kate sipped her drink and watched the clouds thin to ragged banners against an endless sheen of grey light. A pair of wild ducks lifted from the estuary, squabbling amicably.

'It's not too hot? Not too much chilli?'

'No, it's good.'

They ate in silence. After the fish, Phillip sucked down a large bowl of ice cream while Kate sat out on the veranda with yesterday's paper. Gunfire came out of the room behind her; jagged peripheral leaps of colour indicated an American movie in progress while a sweep of headlights below meant that Steve and Alistair were back from their weekend in the Grampians. She knew Anita would be home too, would be sitting in front of the nature program on the ABC. Kate felt a momentary twinge of lust, followed by guilt. Anita didn't really have a hairy face, just the slightest fuzz of blonde down across her cheeks which grazed Kate's in delicious prickly bursts. She could ring her, invite her over or go over there herself… She glanced in through the window, where two men appeared to be hitting each other over the head with guns. No. She needed to break down this sullen wall.

She went inside, waited for the ad break then reached for the remote. 'You've still got the guitar. There's plenty of musicians in this place…'

'This place sucks.' Phillip didn't take his eyes from the screen, where a thin blonde woman silently extolled the virtues of a new laundry liquid.

Kate snapped her off. 'It was your decision to leave school.'

'School was shit.'

Kate opened her mouth. My father left school at fourteen. All his life he wanted an education but stuck in dead-end jobs with five kids… She closed it again.

It had taken considerable persuasion to get the local Work for the Dole coordinator to accept Phillip on one of the revegetation crews. 'He's from out of town, a late starter…'

He had finally agreed to give Phillip a go. 'You owe me big time for this, Katie. You owe me a night at the pub.'

Mick Cox was a good bloke who meant well. Nevertheless, Kate had winced a bit. She'd never seen this government's schemes for the unemployed as anything less than slave labour, or a means of social control, and here she was, whole-heartedly embracing them out of expediency.

Phillip reached for the remote; she snatched it out of reach.

'You'll learn new skills, you'll meet other people…'

'At least it'll be better than that thing you and Mum made.' Phillip propped himself on one elbow. 'That looks like crap.'

Kate laughed. 'So you've seen the sculpture garden?'

'Yeah, Mum took me to see it. The paint's worn off everything and someone's attacked the biggest one with a hammer. The council reckons they might get rid of the whole thing.'

Kate dredged up a remnant from her one abortive year of English lit.: 'I am Ozymandias, King of Kings. Look upon my works, ye mighty, and despair.'

'What's that?'

'Just some crappy poetry from the olden times, when your mother and I were young.'

'At least you and Mum got paid properly. You didn't have to do it on the dole.'

'Things were easier then,' Kate said, thinking back. It seemed inconceivable that one New Year's Eve she and Venice had danced all night and as they walked down Barkly Street at five in the morning carrying their shoes, a man had handed Venice a slightly wilted mauve rose or that one night, wasted on speed, they had screen-printed two hundred T-shirts emblazoned with 'Capitalism is a Bipolar Disorder'.

She sat herself down in the armchair and thrust the remote under a cushion. 'You'll have to tell them you've changed your name. On all the forms I had to fill in, I put you down as Raphael.'

'Raphael's a stupid name. It sucks.'

'It's a beautiful name…' Kate stopped herself. We chose that name the morning you were born. Venice was exhausted after all the blood and tearing but we watched the dawn slowly open up the sky from the window of that public hospital ward. There was a big heraldic streamer of cloud, placenta red, right in front of us.

'Let's call him Raphael, after the archangel of healing, because right now, I need some healing.'

And there was also the painter, of course, the man who made all that delicate amazing art. She had always liked him. Phillip we just tacked on the end, after my mother's father, thinking that it might make the old bitch finally talk to me again. Some hope.

Kate got to her feet. 'It's all right. Your mother started life as Rosemary. If you want to be Phillip, be Phillip. To a certain extent we all make ourselves up as we go along.' She pointed out the window, over the estuary. 'You see over there? That's where you'll be working. What do you think those are?'

'What?' Phillip heaved himself up. 'Where?' He squinted at the long scrapes on the side of the hill Kate indicated, the lesions which darkness had almost overtaken. 'It looks like the tracks of some great big animal that tried to get up the hill and kept slipping down.'

Kate laughed. 'Not bad. They're made by a bulldozer. Know what it was doing there?'

'No. What?'

'When the first European settlers cut down all the trees on the hill, the rabbits more or less took over. When it was decided to replant the hill, which is what you'll be doing, something had to be done about the rabbits. But nothing worked: not baits, not poisons, not traps, nothing.

There were just too bloody many. In the end, they got the bulldozers in to dig up the burrows, to see if they could disrupt the breeding pattern…'

'And did it?'

'No way! So, in the end, you know what they did?'

'What?'

'They blew them up with gelignite!'

'Bullshit!'

'No bullshit. I had fur floating past my windows for weeks. Anytime I felt hungry, I'd just go outside, grab a rabbit and stick it in the oven.'

Phillip was silent. In the distance, a kookaburra's manic cackle zipped up the day.

'All those dead Aborigines,' he said, after a moment. 'They must be laughing themselves sick.'

'Yep.'

They stood there a little longer, not saying anything. Kate saw reflected in the glass all the phantom genes Venice couldn't claim or name: the broad, fleshy cheeks, the eyes which were almost black. Were there some other traits, less visible, only beginning to surface now: melancholy, bitterness, a tendency to self-destruction? No. Phillip's history began with Venice and herself, two soiled and mucky adults seeking redemption through a child untarnished by the world. Their care, haphazard, slipshod and wavering, had never matched the expectations placed upon him.

She watched her reflection slide its arm around Phillip and say, 'You better get to bed pretty soon. You've got an early start tomorrow. Don't forget your safety boots.'

'Yes, *Mum*.' Phillip shrugged out of her grasp. As Kate turned away, from the window, he tapped her casually on the shoulder. 'That shirt's cool.'

'This?' Kate stared down at Che Guevara, at the face once present on a thousand placards but which was now just some advertising boy's wet dream. She had seen the famous photo, taken just after Che was murdered by the – she remembered now – Bolivian army, in which he had been laid out like the martyred Christ. Venice had shown it to her, then shown her Mantegna's *Crucifixion* and pointed out the similarities between the images.

Impulsively, Kate peeled off the shirt. 'You want it? You take it.'

'No, I didn't mean…'

'Go on, take it. Let's swap.' Kate stood there in her dingy sports bra, holding out the shirt.

'Okay.' The dragon flexed and undulated as Phillip stripped of obligingly. 'You're sure you don't mind?'

'No, it's the wrong colour for me. I should have bought the green. You don't mind wearing pink?'

Phillip gave her a pitying look.

'Oh, well, then…fine.' Kate went into her bedroom and examined the effect. She had seen this range of T-shirts down in the town somewhere. It was called 'Porn Queen'. She strutted playfully for a moment, sticking out her chest then threw her leather jacket over the T-shirt. She stuck her thumb out jauntily. She would mention this when she rang Venice in a few days' time. She would wear the shirt into Mick Cox's office, when she went for a report on Phillip's progress, and see whether she got a reaction.

Clothes were part of a person's history, as much as love affairs, music and parking fines. The Labour politician who had opened the sculpture garden had worn a red suit with enormous shoulder pads, red spike heels, a frilly blouse and pink – pink! – pantyhose.

'Fashion victim!' hissed Venice as soon as the woman emerged from her government car. 'What's she trying to do? Is this some Power Dressing meets New Wave fantasy?'

Kate ran water in the sink then walked around the house switching off the lights. It wasn't too late to call Anita.

The Labour politician had made a short but earnest speech, stressing the collaborative efforts of the group and Venice's inspired artistic guidance. 'I just think it's so good that young people like yourselves are being given the opportunity to see the outcome of your creativity in the form of this wonderful garden,' she had gushed.

Now there was a survivor, a woman who had retained the faith of her electorate even after the government's calamitous defeat, then lain low during the years of opposition and re-emerged, in formal but flowing beige and black, to hold the portfolio of Urban Planning and Development.

There had been a plaque, Kate recalled, as she hung up the tea towel to dry and watched the tiny wink of light from the fire spotters' tower on the hill. A plaque commemorating their achievement, set into a small patch of concrete, stating the year and the name of the scheme under which they had been employed. Director: Venice de Mer.

Sic transit gloria, thought Kate, but it hurt her all the same, to think of that youthful energy turning into a pile of tin, to imagine *Ball and Chain* weeping streaky, ferrous tears. She would never go back, although the park which housed the garden was located in the same suburb where Venice had always lived, first in group houses and occasional squats, and now, in vibrant semi-squalor in an unrenovated art deco-style flat. Kate wanted to remember the garden as it was on that day twenty-one years ago, each small plucky artwork carefully displayed in that triangular oasis of grass and shade between a whores' beat and a strip of shops featuring cut-price carpet and panel beating.

She could no longer recall the names of any of the other group participants but she remembered Venice and herself setting out the trays of utilitarian glasses and taking the cans of VB and casks of wine from the fridge on the day of the opening. They were still at the stage of their relationship when lust is molecular, when every particle of the other person is magnetic and amazing. They had been drinking a bottle of French champagne, purchased with what was left of the grant money, and were already a bit pissed. Venice had nicked herself cutting cheese into cubes and Kate had poured wine over the cut finger then gently sucked it before wrapping it in a fragment of rag.

'You'll always be around to patch me up, won't you?' asked Venice, in a voice husky with nausea and fright.

This is what Kate remembered as she switched off the kitchen light and gazed out to the invisible hills which next spring would be crusted with a cloud of saplings, tentative as scabs.

porthole

It had tried to rain overnight but failed. A pall of sea mist obscured all shape and detail until the sun burned through, mid-afternoon. The ridge above the estuary emerged first, shaking off its dank coat while vapour still pooled below.

Sometime later, a woman parked a small grey car in front of the house with the porthole. An imaginary cat skipped down the path to meet her.

'You should get a pet for company.' That is what well-meaning friends had told her when she had announced she was moving to the country.

The house looked straight down to the distant ocean and she regarded it without interest then fumbled in the letter box for the day's mail. There was the first phone bill, which would be practically nothing, and a readdressed item for her husband. She stood for a moment looking at the envelope which bore the stately initials of a law book company and had the urge to throw it on the ground or tear it in two but instead she placed it neatly behind the phone bill and carried it inside.

After six weeks, the house still had the musty, shut-up smell she had noticed when she arrived with the real estate agent, but she thought of it now as a presence. She threw the mail on the pale pine kitchen table and climbed the stairs.

Through the porthole of the room in which she had chosen to sleep, the sea was round and blank as an indifferent eye. She moved to the small sound system and released Bessie Smith's voice. '…there's trouble taking place in the lowlands tonight…there's trouble to make a poor girl wonder where she'll go…'

The woman removed the beige cashmere scarf, the cream knitted cotton sweater and cream linen slacks. She kicked off her low-heeled shoes and felt a vague sense of accomplishment. She lay on the bed in her bra and pants and closed her eyes. When she took the job, it had seemed like a good idea.

'Unfortunately, we don't have a position currently available which is commensurate with your experience,' the young woman at the employment agency had said. 'Nothing at your skill level.'

'That doesn't matter.'

She had already known that gardening and a reading group were not going to fill her time. The position in the bookshop paid poorly but was pleasant in a numbing kind of way. It also fulfilled another admonition of the well-meaning friends: 'You should try to get out more.' Customers came in for cookbooks and self-help manuals and birthday gifts for their children: the time she didn't have to spend thinking was another gift.

But the job had its complications: getting out meant that she had to explain her history. To celebrate the end of her first week, Paul, the manager, had opened a bottle of wine and she had sat around companionably enough with him and the young girl Rebecca then had pleaded a headache.

Friday evenings: these had once been, simultaneously, culmination and anticipation. She and Harold had rarely joined the stream of dutiful end-of-week shoppers. On Friday evenings, they went to a movie or to a meal at one of their favourite restaurants, using the time to acknowledge the triumphs and hardships of their respective working weeks as well as celebrating what stretched before them. And Friday evenings were always about sex, the tingling possibility…

The woman roused herself with a soft groan from the bed. The evening, dark as a shroud, had filled all windows and the porthole. She drew the blinds out of city-dwelling habit then dressed in faded jeans and a white cotton shirt. Clothes mattered to her less than they ever had, the expensive items painstakingly picked out in her previous life left unpacked or discarded in dirty piles after she had worn them. The imaginary cat arched and purred around her legs and she aimed a kick as she descended the stairs. She hated cats.

Upstairs, Bessie Smith's voice ran a husky outline around the smooth-polished stones glimmering outside in their surround of raked gravel. She picked up the envelope carefully as if it were a knife. She thought that she had cancelled all Harold's mail but this had got through, had penetrated her fragile new shell. The address was Californian. She would have to send them an email letting them know.

She scrambled some eggs, drank some more wine, which was more effective than all the sleeping pills the doctor prescribed, then lay down on the bed.

Sometime during the night she woke, turned, reached out, but found only the pillow, a smooth, flat twin to her own; then she slept again.

yin and yang

The first thing Phillip heard when he arrived at Steve and Alistair's old place was the music. He tasted the stale rum from last night and smelt his unwashed hair and skin. He'd slept through the alarm and got up in a hurry. He had put everything he needed, the tools and the timber, in the back of the ute yesterday, so that was no drama. He had pulled on the clothes he found closest to hand, the ones he'd worn to play in last night, then driven the half kilometre down the ridge.

He recognised the singer's voice. Kate liked to play her sometimes, on old scratchy vinyl LPs. He trudged up the path bisecting the Japanese garden which he always thought looked like a desert and knocked on the door. When there was no answer, he knocked again. He turned to leave, pleased to have this part of the morning aborted and looking forward to returning to bed, although cash in hand was always useful.

He was halfway down the path, humming a fragment of the tune, when he felt a gape of air behind him.

'They're not here any more.'

'Beg yours?' Shit, she looked like he felt, hair sticking out like a scarecrows and the sun chiselling grooves around her eyes.

She was staring at him as though he was something from outer space. 'The two guys who used to live here.' She had a strange accent, Aussie mixed with something else. 'They're not here any more.'

'What? No…' He was impatient with her now. 'I've come to do the floor.'

'Oh.'

'The bathroom floor.' He saw her slowly get it together. 'You're Mrs Pearce?'

She winced a little. 'Mira.'

He saw the name as a streak of silvery light. It suited her, fine and sinewy, like a filament of high tensile wire or a string on a guitar. 'I went and stood up on some high old lonesome hill,' the music lamented behind her as he held out his hand.

'Phillip.' He followed her into the kitchen, where she stood looking around as though she had never seen it before.

Mira couldn't remember phoning anyone. That's right, she hadn't. Someone at the general store had mentioned a young bloke who could do the repairs the two previous owners hadn't got around to. 'Real good work, not too pricey, no worries.' In a place like this, you probably took your chances but this kid looked capable enough, with his big, square-knuckled hands and dark eyes above cheek bones which told her he wasn't from the local gene pool. He looked as though he would be strong.

'I'll show you where to get started.'

He followed her through what he supposed was the living room, bare except for some still unpacked cartons. A single photo framed in streamlined silver showed Mrs Pearce holding a bunch of snowy freesias and wearing a white suit and a smile like a core of light. The broad-shouldered man next to her had dark brown skin sheened with fire. Yin and yang: this is what Phillip thought when he saw that photo.

'I'll leave you to it.' Mira climbed the stairs, where light poured in a sickly yellow haze though the porthole.

She felt groggy and tired. You could sleep and sleep and still wake unrefreshed. She caught sight of herself in the mirror and almost laughed out loud: a mad woman or a clown in a fright wig. No wonder he had stared.

The bed beckoned but she didn't lie down. The boy might have a question and it would be embarrassing if he found her there. Bessie Smith had moved on several tracks so she brought her back to 'Backwater Blues'. She played it through twice before pressing Stop, then showered perfunctorily in the en suite, dressed and went downstairs.

Phillip, working in the bathroom, got irritated at having to listen to the same song. On his way out to the ute to get a hammer, he couldn't resist saying casually, 'Good music. She was a real original, wasn't she, Bessie Smith? Do you think we could hear the whole CD?'

Mrs Pearce looked surprised that he would know who Bessie Smith was. Now that she was better equipped to face the day, he could see that she had once been quite good-looking.

She frowned sharply, looked at him for several seconds then laughed. 'Of course.'

As she turned towards the stairs he said, 'Bessie died because a hospital for white people wouldn't let her in after she had a car accident.'

She regarded him thoughtfully. 'Oh, I think that story's been proved apocryphal. The accident happened but the hospital was a fabrication by a white person wanting to draw attention to the evils of segregation in the South.'

She played the CD and the music unfurled around Phillip like the petals of a dark flower. Last night he had played an old Leadbelly song and some chick had asked him later if it was an original composition. She was coming on to him but he hadn't wanted to know about her. After Ebony had kicked him out, he'd gone home with different chicks a couple of times but he was over that, at least for a while. Chicks might say they just wanted sex but they always wanted something else as well. For a while, he might just peel the banana.

The music finished. There was a thin eerie silence.

He looked up to find her standing in the doorway.

'Would you like a coffee?' She made it in a tall Danish plunger and presented it in a mug Phillip knew was different from clunky Safeway shit. She sat across the table, looking at him in an intense kind of way that made him uneasy; then the words came out like bullets from a gun. '"Backwater Blues" was my husband's favourite song.'

'It's a great song,' he replied lamely. He'd finish his coffee, get back to work and get away as quick as he could. He felt sorry for the lady but what could he do? He hoped that she wouldn't start bawling but suddenly she jumped up and poured more coffee before he could refuse.

'We met in Seattle, when I was working in the States.'

'There's some great bands come out of there.' He stopped, thinking he sounded disrespectful and also immature, but she just laughed.

'We were a bit old for grunge. We had a different kind of life.' Pain crossed her face.

Mira was remembering a night almost five years ago. Carmine, that spoilt African princess, had given her father and Mira tickets for the ballet, as a fifth anniversary present. Mira knew that where she was concerned, the gift was a grudging one: Carmine was never going to like her. But it had been a perfect night. The San Francisco Ballet didn't often come to this part of the world and it rarely performed that sugary old classic, *Sleeping Beauty.* The waiter at the restaurant at which they had dined, on learning of the occasion, had returned unexpectedly with a small cake decorated with five fizzing wands of light. Harold had been embarrassed then laughed, as people at the nearby tables applauded. There was always a slight reserve in his manner when they were out in public, a guardedness which hurt her but which she nevertheless understood. That night, as at certain other times, it had almost disappeared and afterwards they had rushed home from the theatre eager as teenagers and fallen into bed...

Mira became conscious that the boy was looking at her expectantly and felt a flash of anger. What would he know about these things? Then she realised she was being unfair. It wasn't his fault that he was young. She forced a smile. 'You're obviously interested in music.'

'I play a bit, and sing. Just in pubs around here.'

'Anything in particular?'

'A bit of everything: blues, ballads, some sixties R&B. I do a few Jeff Buckley covers and some of my own stuff.' He felt inhibited discussing his writing. He didn't want her getting the idea he thought he was a bloody poet or something. He finished his coffee and stood up. 'Thanks.'

'You're welcome.' Mira smiled and this time it wasn't pasted on. He was past being a boy but he still had everything before him.

All afternoon as he planed and sawed, she kept the music up. He was grateful 'Backwater Blues' didn't make an appearance but there were plenty of other things he knew. Once he thought he heard her singing along to 'House of the Rising Sun'. There were places in the States that interested him, such as Chicago and New Orleans, but he didn't want to bother her with questions. Her past hurt her, that was obvious, and she was trying to grow a skin over it.

He said goodbye almost tersely and told her he would be back to finish the job tomorrow. 'Do you mind if I leave the ute here?'

'You're not playing tonight?'

'No.' He couldn't be stuffed going out, either, but if he changed his mind, Kate would loan him her car.

He trudged up the hill. It was April but there was still plenty of light about. Big silver clouds raced towards the horizon and the air smelt damply of woodsmoke and fungi. He forgot all about her as he walked, engrossed as he was in plans of revenge and vituperation regarding Ebony, and wondering if he should send a demo tape to the new place in Port Fairy, but when he got back to Kate's and she asked him about his day, he mentioned the widow.

'She's pretty lonely. Do you think we could extend some traditional country hospitality?'

Kate laughed. She knew all about that. Hospitality was usually extended to couples with children. It had been hard for her when she first came here. A few men had made overtures but when she made it clear she wasn't interested, word had got around. People made allowances for Anita, that wholesome local girl, and now that she and Kate were quite visibly a pairing, things were easier. Still, why should she subject another woman to the same thing? 'Sure, invite her over for dinner.' She half-hoped the woman would refuse. Widow. It had an ominous, old-fashioned sound. Later in the evening, she relayed Phillip's information to Anita.

'Oh, the poor lady. Of course we should invite her over.'

Kate kissed her and wondered what it would be like to have a pure stream of goodness flowing through your veins. As she took the dinner from the oven, music issued from the room which Phillip had recently reoccupied. She really ought to talk about this girl but he had shown no inclination to discuss her. First love could be a tricky thing and he had been the one rejected. Let him go, for the time being; perhaps he needed to write some songs.

She set the table. 'Tucker's ready.'

Anita came in from the vegetable garden, took down two wineglasses and a beer glass. Meaty steam rose from the plates as magpies flew home to rest, letting loose last flights of notes against a lemon and indigo sky. Rays from the descending sun speared bands of cloud. Phillip switched off the television. A bell of yellow light enclosed them while they ate.

in the doorway

Mira slept badly that night. She took a tablet but it didn't help much. When the boy arrived, she was upright but sluggish and totally unprepared for his invitation.

'Dinner? Well…' Mira tried to think of a way to refuse politely. He seemed a likeable kid but she didn't want to spend an entire evening with him. And who were these other people he had mentioned?

'Kate's your mother?'

He laughed. All these years of questions about their relationship and he still hadn't found a satisfactory answer.

'She's kind of my stepmother. She lived with my mother and brought me up, probably more than my mother did.'

'Oh.' Then this other woman…

'Anita's who Kate lives with now.' He laughed, a bit self-consciously. 'I know, it's complicated.'

'Well…' Mira wasn't prejudiced. When you worked in publishing, you came into contact with gay people all the time, and even Harold, that conservative attorney-at-law, had played squash with a colleague who lived openly with an interior designer. However, being unusual didn't mean this stepmother and her friend would be interesting. Perhaps they were on some homespun, back-to-the-land trip, old hippie leftovers from the seventies.

Phillip, seeing her hesitate, and thinking of the pile of books he had seen on the table, said, 'Kate's an author, sort of.'

Mira smiled. Did Kate compose rhyming verse about whales for a local writers' group? Well, if nothing else, the evening might provide material for the phone calls she hadn't been making to city friends and the emails she had neglected to send. 'All right. Thanks. That would be nice.' She established the details then let him get on with his work.

Despite everything, she felt a small surge of anticipation. She even bothered to select clothes then drove down to the town and bought a reasonably expensive bottle of wine; she hoped that these women were not so homespun that they didn't drink. She put on music, a dreadful old disco compilation which had belonged to Harold and kept him company during his years as a young husband and father and which caused an outcry from the bathroom.

'I should be getting time-and-a-half if I have to listen to KC and the Sunshine Band.' He stood in the doorway, grinning, a corkscrew of wood shaving trapped in his dark hair.

Mira laughed. 'Suffer.' In 1978, her younger sister had driven around in a beaten-up Ford Escort with a sticker on the rear window proclaiming DISCO SUX.

'Take a lunch break. I promise to turn it off.' She put on Nina Simone and made him an omelette. 'So this is what you do for a day job?'

He shrugged. 'I do this, I do that. Carpentry, tiling, whatever. It pays the bills.'

'Variety's a good thing.' It sounded like a precarious way to earn money but he was young and of another time and place to herself. Both her parents had suffered during the Depression but they had been able to afford education for their children. Even when you were female, being an arts graduate in the sixties, gave you options. But perhaps this boy, Phillip, didn't care about careers and status.

She made some coffee and asked whether he had always lived around here. She heard about his early life, about being dragged around from pillar to post by his beautiful erratic mother and her succession of male and female lovers, about the steadfast Kate who took up the slack when things got out of control, his boredom with school and his lack of regrets about his limited education. She even heard about his girlfriend, or rather, the ex-girlfriend, that bitch, and agreed that, yes, twenty was much too young to settle down.

'I started to worry she'd get pregnant, you know, accidentally on purpose. Anyway, she got the shits... Do you have kids?'

'I was nearly fifty when I married Harold. He had two children from his first marriage but they were grown up by the time we got together.' Not that Mira ever thought of Carmine as grown up. Paul had disapproved of her – he thought marriage to a white woman would damage his father's career – but he hadn't disliked her personally. Over the years they had negotiated a civilised arrangement; however, she doubted whether she would see him or his family again.

She gazed out the kitchen window at the mild blue sea ruffled with foam. The sun, which had been sailing easily across the mid-afternoon sky, suddenly disappeared, turning the water dingy and the stones in the garden to lead.

It can be as quick as that, Mira thought. It only takes a moment for the light to go. Everything changes. You can be going about your business, having your normal, slightly harried day. The phone rings; everything changes.

She stood up abruptly. She took the boy's mug, with its remaining dark dregs, and swirled them down the sink, as she felt a storm of bitter anger build. 'I have to go now.'

She climbed the stairs, kicked the door shut and threw herself face down on the bed, fists clenched and with an arid burning behind her eyes. The irony of the situation did not escape her: to be surrounded by salty water and not able to produce a single tear. She moaned convulsively then stifled herself, thinking of the kid downstairs. At twenty, your heart could be broken or badly damaged but it would regenerate as surely as a stubborn shoot in fertile soil.

She rolled over and the porthole fixed her with its bleak grey gaze. This was her life now: time moving, always moving but with all light gone. It seemed that for a long time she watched the sea, its futile unfolding motion repeated again and again, until finally her eyes closed against it.

When she woke, the house held the silence of absence and she knew that he had gone. She glanced at the red numbers on the bedside clock. 5.32.

His invitation had been for around six-thirty. Her first thought was to phone and make an excuse, plead a headache, not entirely a lie at the moment, but she thought of the effort the other women would have made on her behalf. Harold would have said that to back out now was both cowardly and churlish.

She showered, dressed and collected the wine from the fridge. She had last-minute second thoughts but remembered the boy standing in the doorway, lightly oiled with sweat, laughingly protesting about music recorded long before he was born. In the end, she drove the small grey car up the hill.

fire. sofa. drink

When Kate first saw her, she thought, this has been a big mistake. She took in the salmon-coloured scarf resting on fawn cashmere, the caramel velvet pants and the soft kid boots. The widow was on the far side of middle age and fine as a race horse. In a previous life, Kate had known some of these subtly understated women: how she hated the arrogance their costume implied. However, the woman was here now and they would just have to make the best of it.

She held out her hand. 'Kate Ahearn.'

Mira recognised her immediately. Eleven years on, the face was rather weather-beaten, the freckles darker, the hair unruly and in need of a cut. But it was the same face the company that Mira worked for then had placed on the inside back cover of a novel it was promoting as authentic and moving. Mira had read the novel expecting the claim to be publishing hype; instead she found a startling new voice. Now she took the proffered hand, feeling the slight roughness of the palm.

The other woman, Anita, was tall, thin to gauntness. She stood behind her lover, her straw-coloured hair framing a face flushed by heat. 'Welcome,' she said.

A rich smell came from the oven. Flames licked the door of a pot-belly stove in the lounge. On the wall above a well-used sofa, someone had pieced together hexagons of dark blue and green silk then framed them. Rugs were spread across oiled floorboards and there were several armchairs which didn't match the sofa. On the other side of the room, wooden chairs arranged themselves around a large table with carved legs. You could feel at home here, thought Mira, and it seemed a long time since she had felt that way about anywhere.

'Take a seat.' Anita placed supermarket dips, olives and biscuits on a low table in front of the fire. 'Would you like a drink?'

'Thanks.' Mira handed her the wine. Fire. Sofa. Drink. You could build an entire civilisation on these things. 'This is a nice place,' she said, then realised how banal she sounded.

'We like it.' Kate Ahearn looked at her speculatively.

But you don't like me, Mira thought. She was familiar with disenfranchised intellectuals who despised the middle class. But what's your claim to superiority? Your talent dried up like a spring shower in the sun. She sipped the wine.

Phillip came out of his room wearing a pair of those trousers with multiple pockets young people liked and a black T-shirt with cut-off sleeves. 'No problems finding us?'

Mira smiled. He'd sensed the slight strain in the atmosphere and was doing his best to ease it. 'I managed.'

She remembered her behaviour earlier in the day and felt embarrassed but all he said was, 'I finished the job.'

'You finished the bathroom floor?' Anita handed him a beer and the conversation flowed into safe domestic channels: bathrooms, houses, home renovation, the wide appeal of television programs about home renovation and gardening.

'So what will your next project be? Getting rid of that pile of rubble out the front?' Phillip asked.

'The rubble? Oh, you mean the Japanese garden? I don't know,' Mira laughed. 'It's easy maintenance.'

'Kind of wanky, though, don't you think?' he said, looking slyly sideways at Anita. 'Just the sort of thing you'd expect pooftas to have.'

'Oh, put a sock in it,' she said, good-naturedly.

'Well, it's true,' he needled.

'People are just people as far as I'm concerned.' Anita's light grey eyes, flecked with brown, were serene as she shovelled logs onto the fire. 'The gay/straight stuff's had no influence on me.'

'Oh, bullshit, of course it has.' Kate Ahearn came in from the kitchen and laid a heavy fan of silver on the table. 'If it hadn't been for that "stuff", you wouldn't be doing what you're doing now, or living the life you live. You'd have married some farmer and be stuck at home baking scones for the CWA, having attacks of nerves and wondering what was wrong with you.'

'I suppose you should be grateful, then.' Anita reached over and pinched her gently on the leg.

'Yes, and so should you.'

It was said without hostility but Mira detected an underlying note of exasperation. She caught Phillip's eye. He grinned and gave an almost imperceptible shrug. He must be used to all forms of female verbal sparring, the many subtle gradations of bitchiness and manipulation. He probably understood women quite well.

They watched while Kate carried a large earthenware casserole dish to the table and set it down on a bread board.

'Help yourself,' she invited Mira.

It was spicy lamb, made with nuts and apricots and served with couscous and salad.

Mira drank more wine and watched the flames leap in the stove while she talked about the job at Simon and Schuster which had taken her overseas and the occasional vicissitudes of being an ex-pat. 'Even Melbourne doesn't prepare you for the eternal Seattle drizzle.' It was a relief not to have to explain why she had returned, a relief not to have them ask. She managed to mention Harold quite naturally a couple of times.

Anita had made a self-saucing chocolate pudding and there was good strong coffee. As they lolled in front of the fire once more, she produced a bottle of vintage port.

'Oh, no, please, no!' Mira protested. 'I couldn't fit in another thing!'

The fire refracted the ruby heart of the port in its small crystal glasses. She was afraid she would fall asleep, even though Anita was relating an anecdote about a runaway boa constrictor from the early days of her practice; then Phillip went into his room and came back with his guitar.

'Oh, is there to be entertainment?' Kate Ahearn, who had been reclining on the sofa, propped herself on an elbow.

'I reckon.'

He spent a few moments tuning then launched into something Mira had never heard. The song line was simple, the words above it translucent. They were about the hold a place could have on you, about going away and then returning. They should have been a cliché but they caught Mira and held her. For the first time, she saw the landscape in which she now lived. The heave of blue-green water and trees which bowed to lashing rain: these things could become part of you.

When he finished, the only sound was the low sputter of the flames.

'That's turned out well,' Kate said. 'Have you made it part of your set?'

'I've played it a few times.'

'It's good.' She looked across at Mira. 'I'm Phil's artistic advisor.'

'I'm sure you're very helpful.' The words came out more stiffly than Mira intended. Is this what you did with those lyrical lines which flowed across the page? Do you give them away for this boy to sing in front of drunks? But she said nothing more.

Phillip started into 'Me and Bobby McGee', and Anita joined in with a clear surprising soprano. Kate Ahearn had the voice of a warrior queen, a fierce alto. Mira faltered then found her pitch. Her throat was tight and she was aware of some long unused energy nested in her diaphragm, which was blocked and feeble. Memories of school choir practice from over forty years ago surfaced, of a short, balding fussy little man trying to meld together the voices of thirty tunic-clad girls. She closed her eyes and imagined a silver thread of sound rising through the top of her head.

Phillip heard it. He heard the pure strand of sound rising from the core of her. He began, amazingly, to sing 'Amazing Grace', unsure that he even knew the words, and she followed him, setting up a descant line which climbed over his baritone. Mira opened her eyes and smiled at him. They sang the whole song through and finished together.

'Wow!' exclaimed Anita. 'Are you a churchgoer? They'd love you here with a voice like that!'

'I'm agnostic.' But Mira was pleased. She felt released. Shy too, with his black velvet eyes on her, branding her as an accomplice in a risky escapade. 'Do you know "Here Comes the Sun"?'

He played that, then 'Don't Think Twice, It's All Right', and two songs which she didn't know from later decades. Then, out of nowhere, keeping his eyes down and fixed on the belly of his instrument, he struck the first notes of 'Backwater Blues'. Those long fingers, which could hold a hammer and plane a virgin plank of wood, coaxed a different sound from the song than Mira had ever heard. '…they rowed a little boat about five miles across the pond…'

He looked up and a sudden flame of heat swept Mira from her groin to face. Ridiculous. She should be angry at his presumption but here she was stabbed with lust. Ridiculous and obscene. He was one-third her age. When he was born, she was already senior editor with the firm which had published his stepmother's novel; she had been a well-travelled homeowner, with an investment property as well, and three significant relationships behind her. What she was feeling was an aberration, degrading and disloyal. She pulled up memories of Harold: his arm thrown across a sheet early in the morning, dining out with him under the stars on a rooftop restaurant in New Orleans, photos of his grid iron career in college.

She waited until the boy had finished then spoke in a pleasant, even tone. 'That was lovely, Phillip, but it's past this old lady's bedtime.' She thanked the other women for the meal and the enjoyable evening and then they saw her out. She was slightly the worse for the wine but the car rolled down the hill obediently.

Phillip, left behind at the fire, thought that he had offended her. He had intended the song as a gift but had only caused her further pain. He poured himself a Jim Beam and Coke and considered phoning Ebony, but it was almost midnight. Forget it. He'd stuff that up as well. When Anita and Kate came inside, he was leaning over the guitar and writing something down on paper.

'Well, she's still a very attractive woman. She must have been gorgeous when she was young.'

'You think so, do you?' Anita grinned and ran water in the sink.

Phillip said nothing. He remembered the strong column of her throat, the way she had smiled at him when they sang and the voice which sounded like the morning of a summer day.

balcony

Kate waited almost a week to return the scarf. That capricious twist of coral silk had slipped from Mira's tipsy neck and wedged behind a sofa cushion. Kate found it when she was tidying up and could have dropped it off several times, going to or from work, but she chose not to. However, Anita was away for a week at a conference in Brisbane and Phillip had been hired as part of a crew building the new motel in town. It was coming into that time of the year when business at the servo was slack because the tourists either stayed at home or went north. Kate had time on her hands.

On Saturday afternoon, she walked down the hill and opened Mira's front gate. The stones lay still as sepulchres in the front garden but the sun was out and there was a glinting sea. The voice of some long-dead diva poured in crackly rapture through the open door.

'Anyone home?'

There was a second of silence then John Cargher started talking about Budapest in 1936.

'I'm up here.'

Kate raised her eyes to the small first-floor balcony which led off the main bedroom.

Mira had been lying down, with the radio on and the door to the balcony open. She saw Kate hold up the pinkish-gold streamer of silk then flutter it like a tournament pennant. Mira was irritated. The letter box would have done.

She came down the stairs and through the front door, intending to thank Kate and send her on her way but something about her expression, a fault line of loneliness running through the dykey bravado, changed her mind. 'I read your novel.'

'Did you?' Kate laughed. 'You must have been one of the thirteen people who did.'

'Do you have time to stop for a while?'

'Hey, I'm not going anywhere.'

Mira's friend Averil had sent a bottle of champagne as a house-warming gift so it was exhumed from the fridge and placed next to some Safeway cheddar and Salada crackers. Kate was pleased Mira made no apology for this proletarian snack.

They sat out on the balcony, listening to the fragment of Puccini which always closed *Singers of Renown*. A jet moved slowly up the sky, leaving behind a white scar of vapour which widened and thinned.

'That novel was shortlisted for the Vogel. Why did you stop writing?'

Kate shrugged. If she stood up and craned her neck, she could see the servo, its twinkly green and gold logo and all the prosaic busyness which went with it.

'You've got to put bread on the table. God knows, writing won't do that.'

'Well, yes...' Mira was unconvinced but she chose not to probe further.

Kate added, grudgingly, 'I wrote that novel as a kind of catharsis, after some heavy relationship fallout. Very deep emotion, profound grief or anger, sometimes needs that outlet.'

'I suppose so.' Mira's gaze followed the jet trail in the sky. Her profile carved the air. 'Although, sometimes, in that situation, you're lucky if you can feel anything.'

'That's how it was for you?'

Mira smiled. The past tense was a nice touch. 'I don't remember anything of the first six months after Harold died.'

A slight exaggeration. There had been Carmine's tantrum about the house: 'Daddy always said he would leave it to us.' There had been the uneasiness of some of the couples with whom she and Harold had been friends; then one of the husbands, a soon-to-be-retired doctor, had started writing her poetry. When she heard about this, Averil flew from Sydney, held Mira for moments at the airport, then bathed her in steadying common sense: 'If you don't want the house, let her have it – but don't give it to her. She can buy it.' She had inspected a couple of the sonnets. 'These are awful. You'd better come home.'

But home had proved to be an illusion. After ten years, the old familiar roads didn't lead to the places Mira once knew. What had been a favourite restaurant now sold discount furniture. Two young women specialising in tarot reading and astrology occupied the premises of a former antiquarian bookshop. Many of the people from that time had moved away or were leading lives she couldn't enter. A few of them were dead. Mira knew it was unrealistic to expect things not to have changed but the city made her feel like a refugee. She had nothing to lose when she saw an advertisement for the property in the seaside town where she had spent childhood holidays: 'Three spacious bedrooms (one with en suite), modern kitchen, landscaped garden, ocean views.'

Mira watched Kate upend the last of the bubbles then produce a bottle of Chardonnay from her backpack. The wine and the sunlight glazed the ocean; the waves were brittle shells, breaking then reforming.

'This woman…' Mira assumed it was the charismatic artist, Phillip's mother. 'You must have loved her very much.'

Kate sat facing into the breeze, both hands cradling her glass, watching the scurry of the fishing boats. The wine, bought on special last week, tasted yellow and stale. 'It was like a bloody grand opera at times. She got into drugs, we started tearing each other apart, then she left.'

'Mine were never like that. I always called it quits before we got to the tearing apart stage.'

'There was never anyone that serious for you?'

'Serious, yes, but not that serious. Not until Harold. I'm older than you…' Mira carefully set down her glass. 'You've got to remember, I belong to that generation of experimentation, first flower power, then feminism. All those ideas about true love, about there being one person for the rest of your life, they were considered at best a bad joke or at worst shocking lies, when I was young. They weren't supposed to be relevant any more. That's why it was all the more…shocking, I suppose, is the only way to describe it, when I found out someone could be everything to me.'

'And when that goes…' Quite recently, Kate had been cleaning out some cupboards and had come across an old shoebox containing her letters to Venice, which had been eventually returned to her after innumerable requests. Kate couldn't believe the letters. She had almost shoved them into the stove but the vicious old dragon of memory stayed her hand. 'I can't live with you but if I'm apart from you I will surely…'

Kate shook her head. She wasn't going to give Mira the pleasure of hearing about it. Instead she said, 'I did the whole non-monogamous thing when I was younger. I guess I'm your descendant, although if you're gay, you're considered deviant to begin with. Sometimes the need to be seen as undeviant makes us conform. We run around demanding the right to marry or else we embrace suffocating monogamy.'

'As you have?'

Kate was silent for a moment. 'Anita's a pure person. She always acts from integrity. There aren't many people around like that.'

'But you don't love her.'

'Not in the way you're talking about – but there are worse things in life than companionship. How many people do you know who have ended up with the love of their life? There's no shame in settling for something else.'

There was something intractable here, a stone wall which would be difficult to scale, nevertheless, Mira couldn't resist trying. 'I guess companionship is what most relationships settle into, eventually. The ones which don't fail, that is. I don't see it as second best necessarily…'

Kate laughed drily. 'That's very magnanimous.' The sourness she tasted was not just the wine. The whole conversation was moving, treacherous as a sudden shelf of reef beneath silky blue water, to a place she didn't like. There was the danger she would start talking about the draft of the second novel she had resting in a desk drawer.

The gabble of some self-important Radio National commentator filled the silence between them as she shouldered the backpack. 'I've got some things to do at home. Thanks for the savouries. We'll catch up with you sometime.'

After she left, Mira remained on the balcony, berating herself. There had always been this insistent quality within her, a striving for precision that made her superb in her work but sometimes translated awkwardly to her interaction with other human beings. It was something Harold had realised, early on. 'You're an all or nothing girl. Not everybody's so intense.'

Now she had probed a fissure, opened up a privacy which was someone's self-preservation. And there had been something malicious in it, a secret delight born from the power of being able to twist the knife in a tender place. 'Sometimes you're lucky if you can feel anything.'

For she was jealous, no doubt about it. She envied Kate her companionship and all the mundane pleasures which were part of it: to be able to discuss bathroom repairs, to be able to say, with a devastating lack of emphasis, 'We'll catch up with you sometime.'

Mira poured the final glass of wine as a murky apricot pall of cloud dragged itself across the sky then shredded darkly behind a knot of gulls flying into chill blue air. She shivered. She realised she was crying. She must move, must act, because to sit here rancid with self-pity was a terrible thing. As she bent to pick up the now-empty bottle, the rising moon painted the stones in the garden with malevolent light. Those flat perfect mocking stones…

Mira hurled the bottle and it exploded into a thousand shards of scattered light. She fled into the bedroom, knocked the tower of CDs left stacked on top of the speaker to the floor and knelt, frantically sifting, until she found Bessie Smith. 'I went and stood up on some high old lonesome hill…that's when the blues told me to pack my things and go…'

She would go, she would leave this dismal little backwater, but first she had to pick up the pieces and this was what Phillip saw as he drove up the hill on his way home. At first he thought the pale thing was some kind of animal, down on all fours dementedly digging, but when he realised who it was, throwing the rocks into a pile and spewing dirt into the night sky, he stopped, slammed the ute door and vaulted the low fence. She saw him and momentarily straightened. Her nails were bloody, there was a weal of blood along a bare arm and her shirt was smeared with dirt.

'I'm gardening!' she laughed.

Phillip heard madness in that laugh. As she bent down once more to the crater she had made, he locked his arms around her waist and dragged her back. She fought him, turning and striking uselessly at his shoulders while she heaved and sobbed. He carried her upstairs to the bed, turned off the music, stripped her naked then covered her. He waited, gently stroking her face and hair, then she dropped a guiding hand, so that he slipped in easily as a fish, a patient swimmer carried by an urgent racing tide.

seven crayfish at christmas

Purcell knew who she was, the dyke who lived out of town on the hill with the vet; nevertheless, that didn't stop him dropping the crayfish with the purple ribbon twining its abdomen, onto her table at the pub. 'There ya go!' He stood back, grinning.

She didn't scream or carry on the way some women would but he hadn't expected her to. She just sat there, watching the prehistoric thing clack and slither across the orange laminex. Then she threw it at him.

'Uh…hey!'

It landed on the floor, where it scrabbled dismally until Purcell retrieved it and put it back in the hessian sack.

'That's no way to treat a cray!'

She regarded him coolly. Kate knew who he was, the lair of a fisherman who lived out on one of the back roads with the hippy wife who took photos. Their elder daughter painted her toenails black and was pregnant to some loser who had done time for breaking and entering. The younger one liked horses and had so far managed to stay out of trouble. Kate supposed that a man like this would be disappointed at not having sons, someone he could go fishing with or take to the footy. The sack buckled and heaved.

'Are you playing Santa Claus? What else have you got in there?'

Purcell winked. He raffled the cray, which was won by that red-nosed old bastard Terry Donovan, and afterwards he bought a beer and sat across the table from her. 'So what have you been up to?' he asked, as though he'd known her all his life.

'Not a lot.'

Kate had stopped off to chill before she went home. She had finished work late at the servo, had had to tidy up the mess left by the sixteen-year-old casual put on for the holidays. Out across the bay, on the road which snaked along the cliff top, a spine of headlights signalled the season's first influx of visitors. This happened every year but suddenly it made her depressed.

'Look at that.' She gestured towards the lights. 'It doesn't seem possible that there's so many people in the world.'

Purcell frowned. 'If people want to come down here, they can,' he said brusquely. 'It's good for business.'

'Oh, yes,' said Kate. 'Business.'

This made them both laugh. Purcell supposed that it was a funny thing, people coming from everywhere to look at a group of rocks in the water and look at all the fuss a couple of years back, when one of them fell over. Kate listened with only half an ear: the sixteen-year-old could probably be bullied and cajoled into being an adequate employee but she would have to fire that boofhead Andrew, who kept turning up late. She felt Purcell's curiosity reach across the table but she was used to that. He didn't hold much mystery for her, the town was full of men like him, but she admired his weather-beaten forearms, jewelled with springy gold hairs, resting on the table. They married young, these men, they had their kids young. By the time they reached his age, they were conscious that they had missed out on a few things.

She bought him another beer; she'd heard he liked a drink or three. Purcell sipped in a measured sort of way and looked at the hazel eyes, which were her only pretty feature, really. Ordinarily, he would have launched into the rambling tale about his father kicking the winning goal in the local grand final forty years ago, kicking the ball so hard that it sailed over the cliff, but he suspected that she'd be bored. Instead, he told her about finding the Aboriginal grinding stone, the stone cocooned in the grinder like an egg in a nest. 'Both worn as smooth as silk…'

Words failed Purcell. He'd considered keeping it but in the end his better instincts prevailed and he'd taken it to the district's Indigenous Cultural Officer.

'So I was left without the stone but got to keep a warm inner glow.'

Kate was charmed by the way he sent himself up but wasn't about to let on. She looked around. It had got dark outside and the pub was taking last orders for meals. The rumble of German wrapped itself around a couple of steaks at a nearby table.

'You want to eat?'

'Nah.' Purcell glanced at his watch. He'd run on at the mouth as usual, when he'd had a few. His wife would be waiting with the next instalment about Tanya and her fiancé. Jasmine, his darling, so named because she had been conceived one hot and steamy night under a luxuriant bush of the same name, would have fed the young thoroughbred and the old pony.

Kate watched him cross the street, lit by a single overhead light, moving with conscious care between the groups and couples drifting up from the foreshore. Purcell jangled car keys and looked up. Framed by the dirty yellow window, she was as unsmiling as an idol on a throne but she was in for a surprise. He grinned, put the ute into gear and headed off.

The following evening, Kate came home to find Anita and her black kelpie Sootball chasing two crayfish around the laundry.

'Someone left them in the letterbox!' Anita's patient Calvinist face was flushed. One index finger displayed an angry red indentation. 'Tied up with string! Who would do such a thing?'

Kate grinned. That sneaky bugger. He must have timed it just before Anita got home. The colour of the shells was hardly faded.

She picked one up and placed it gently in the laundry trough. 'No need to freak out. You're used to dealing with animals.'

'I don't usually deal with shellfish.' Anita shut the laundry door firmly and crossed the gravel to the kitchen.

Kate imagined him hauling the crays out of the pot, his freckly, square-palmed hands expertly turning them while he checked their length. She threw the other one in the trough and wondered what he was doing: perhaps crossing the rocking deck of his boat on muscular, gold-furred legs, or back in the pub, first beer of the evening in hand, blue eyes crinkling beneath his cap.

Actually, Purcell had taken out the tinny with the small outboard he kept at the boat shed. He sat with a single line, marooned with his own thoughts, watching the sky change colour. He'd made himself some peanut butter sandwiches and he consumed them as he worried about his daughter. In the early years of his marriage, his wife had made his sandwiches, exotic concoctions featuring smoked salmon and crispy bacon and avocado; now he made his own.

Purcell threw a crust overboard. If you had no education, fishing wasn't a bad choice of livelihood. You weren't a slave to animals the way a farmer was, or a slave to the road, like a truck driver. He caught several small salmon, which he killed quickly and transferred to his sack, then he warmed himself with a thermos of coffee and a piece of chocolate. Purcell had a terrible sweet tooth.

He considered visiting the dyke on the hill but knew that the lanky girlfriend, who looked like a real ball-breaker although people spoke highly of her skill, would be there. Purcell fished until pale aquamarine flamed to mauve and gold. He had a piss over the side then turned the boat to shore, hoping that the girls had been able to use the crays, but in that he was to be disappointed. Their fridge was chockers with food for Christmas so in the end Kate and Anita gave the crays away to Mira down the road.

Kate sat in the Loch Ard Café, idly turning the pages of the *Age* and sipping a breakfast latte. At the next table, a group of Canadians debated whether or not to visit the Wool Museum in Geelong. Of all the tourists who came to the town, Canadians were the daggiest.

Kate looked up as the chair opposite scraped back and Purcell's wife deposited her camera bag on the floor. She gazed at Kate, who waited for her to speak. Celeste: it was a pretentious name, or a name a woman called Wendy might adopt when she took a job in a massage parlour.

Her work was good. Kate had seen the exhibition at the local gallery, frame after frame of vast aching skies above a landscape swept clean of people. The land was peripheral rubble skirting a world of water and air, in which sudden leaps of spray were sucked towards a retreating sun. Someone had suggested to the artist that she make postcard reproductions and sell them in the shops, but she had disdainfully declined. She pressed her hands, palms down, against the table. The Canadians, caps and T-shirts ornamented with maple leaves, tramped towards the counter.

'I never come here. Can you recommend anything?'

'It's all fairly good. Are you vegan?'

'No.'

'Have some eggs, then,' but the woman contented herself with coffee.

Kate gazed past her, through the floor-to-ceiling windows, out to the glassy sea.

'I had an affair with a woman once.'

'Really?' Kate turned the page and noted the cricket scores, pleased that the Poms were being thrashed.

'Yes. At boarding school. It wouldn't have lasted. I'm not really that way. I wanted a family.'

'They're fine things when they work well.'

Kate examined her curiously. The frazzly hair would have been pretty when she was a teenager but now it just looked dry. She had the sun-damaged skin common to women around here. One of the dark drapey dresses she favoured skimmed her hip bones.

'Have you ever photographed crayfish?' Kate indicated the Leica. 'There's a very nice still life of three crayfish I could direct you to.'

They had been left, inert on a sacrificial white platter, on the veranda. Sootie was a hopeless watch dog. She hadn't barked.

'I don't do still life. I don't do product shots. I don't do advertising.'

'Fair enough.' Kate was bored with her. The woman should either make a scene or go away.

Kate saw that little spunk rat Ebony standing behind the espresso machine and fished some change from her wallet.

'Oh, please,' said the woman. 'Let me pay.'

At that moment, Purcell and a friend were passing along the opposite side of the street. They saw Kate get up from the table and, with gestures neither belligerent nor obscene, indicate her total lack of interest in the idea.

'You better watch out, mate,' the friend said, jovially. 'She'll run off with your missus.'

'Mate, I wouldn't mind as long as they let me join in occasionally.'

That evening, after she finished work, Kate went looking for Purcell. His big commercial boat was tied up at the jetty but he wasn't there.

'You lookin' for Jimmy?' someone asked. 'He's around at Little Bay, mendin' nets.'

She didn't need directions. Halfway across the car park, one of her thongs broke and she kicked them both off then drove out of town and found the track which led down to the inlet nestled between cliffs.

Purcell was out the front of the shed where he kept the tinny, sitting on an upturned red milk crate, patiently drawing filaments of rope together, when she slammed to a stop beside his ute.

'This can't go on,' she called.

He regarded her quizzically. She looked a mess, her hair a sweaty tangle from the drive in the old Subaru and purplish crescents beneath her eyes. Not sleeping well? Something hormonal?

He felt a certain satisfaction as she crossed the tide-slimed area between them. 'What are you talking about?'

'This!' Kate swept her arm in a wild circle. 'All your…donations!'

'Donations.' He looked amused. 'Do you know how much crays are selling for in the shops?'

'Yes,' said Kate, 'and I'm not grateful!' Then her feet went from under her; a ridge of sea rock, weathered to a razor, sliced her arch as she went down. She landed with starfish arms and lay looking up at the hard arc of the sky.

Purcell left his nets. 'Up-sy,' he said, as though speaking to a child. He extended a hand.

Blood streamed from Kate's foot. Purcell handed her a hanky, which surprised her because she hadn't realised she was crying. She leaned on him and they made it across to the shed, then he took a rough towel and went to work, bathing her foot in cold water and dabbing on antiseptic lotion.

'It's just a joke,' he said. 'I've been known to jack people's cars up at parties so that they can't drive off.'

'What?' Kate, light-headed from the fall and the touch of his hands, didn't know what he was talking about.

'The crays.'

'Oh.'

He pressed an adhesive patch firmly over the wound. 'That should do it. It's not as bad as it seems.' He looked up from where he squatted. 'I've got one in the fridge. Have you eaten?'

They ate the cray, breaking its body into segments then cracking the legs for sweet meat, with white bread and butter, iceberg lettuce and a can of Vic each. Afterwards they had Neapolitan ice cream in plastic bowls. Through the meal they talked companionably, like some long-braided couple, about the day's events and about their current problems: Purcell's daughter, Kate's frustration with her job.

Eventually the moon became a distant silver guest.

Purcell piled the dishes in the sink and saw her out. 'Goodbye. Watch your step.'

'You haven't finished the nets...'

'Fuck the nets.' He kissed her in a formal courtly way then closed the door.

The tide had gone out. The rocks were dry. Kate drove up the hill, past windows illuminated by neon flashes from gaudy trees and SEASONS GREETINGS. Tomorrow was Christmas Eve. As she turned into the driveway she saw the Tarago belonging to Anita's sister and brother-in-law. Their three kids ran around, chased by Sootie and Reg, the golden retriever. The adults sat on the veranda with an open bottle of wine and plates of crayfish and salad.

'Where have you been?' Anita called. 'We thought something had happened.'

'Nothing happened,' Kate replied, although she couldn't help limping slightly as she made her way to the back door.

'You're hurt?' Anita put down her glass and descended the steps.

'No. I fell, but I'm all right.'

Kate had had enough of being vulnerable. She escaped upstairs and, with a soft groan of relief, sank onto the bedspread, bought when they were in Thailand a couple of years ago. She pulled off the plaster and flexed her foot experimentally but he had been right, it was nothing much. The clean white mouth of the wound had already puckered shut. In a few days she wouldn't be able to tell that there had ever been anything there.

sea pictures

Kate stood in front of Manet's *Olympia*, which she had managed to locate, despite becoming lost with Venice in the Musée d'Orsay. To see the painting of the naked courtesan, which had so scandalised the art-going public when first exhibited in 1865, had been Venice's ardent wish, announced at breakfast that morning.

'It's a pilgrimage, a sacred quest,' she said, scraping jam from her plate.

Kate, who had woken wanting to take a train to the coast, knew that Venice wasn't up to it so she had settled for this visit to a former railway station, converted by the French into a temple of culture.

All around her, people surged or stood gawking before Renoir, Degas and Morisot. Kate considered Olympia, whose broad peasant face stared levelly back as she reclined wearing feathery mules and a ribbon choker, the tools of her trade. A small black cat arched and hissed and an African maid hovered in the background holding a starburst of flowers.

Kate checked her mobile: nothing from Phillip, nothing from Françoise.

'Oh, there she is!'

Two Japanese beside Kate turned their heads as Venice moved rapidly towards them, legs scissoring in baggy denim and her gauzy black shirt clearly revealing the lacy patterning of the black bra beneath.

'Yep, this is her. Sorry about the wild goose chase. Are you all right?'

'Yeah, fine. I had a fascinating encounter with a charming young attendant on the next floor who spoke five languages.'

'And they were?'

'German, Czech, Russian, French, English.'

'There's a whole history there, wouldn't you say? A fascinating family saga?'

'Possibly, although it sounds like a high price to pay for cultural diversity.'

Venice rocked gently back and forth on her plastic clogs, her eyes half-closed in a worshipful gaze Kate felt obliged to puncture.

'Pornographic.'

'It depends on your perspective. She's a paradox. She looks back at the viewer, instead of contemplating her own beauty, and that's very modern. Manet modelled her on Titian's *Venus of Urbino*, but this chick's no goddess, she's real.'

'Is that so?'

'On the other hand, she's a forerunner of the modern pin-up. She's a bit of a tease, the ultimate whore icon.'

Kate could only suppose that Venice was feeling nostalgic for her own whore past, although she could not recall her having any icons then, apart from heroin. She glanced at a nearby clock. 'Do you want to take a look in the gift shop? This place will close soon. I'll buy you the *Olympia* coffee mug or the *Olympia* T-shirt.'

'You go ahead.' Venice closed her eyes again; she lurched slightly.

Kate caught her and took her to a chair. She sat down then reached into her bag and gave Venice some illegal sips of water.

'You go ahead,' Venice kept repeating. 'I'll be fine. Buy something outrageous. Go on, surprise me.'

Kate checked her mobile again as she hurried towards the glossy books and merchandise. Still nothing from Phillip. She had phoned Venice, rather than sending an email, the previous week, because she wanted to hear shrieks and groans of envy when she nonchalantly announced, 'I'm in Paris,' but all Venice said was, 'Is that Paris, Texas, or Paris, New South Wales?'

Kate had laughed. She could afford to feel magnanimous. She was in Paris, her work on the novel was going well, but then the day before yesterday Venice had turned up, literally, on her doorstep. She had been waiting when Kate arrived back from her first date with Françoise.

'You! How did you get here?'

'Magic carpet.'

'But the air fare?'

'Some of the money Daddy left me is on call, night and day. I called it.'

'You didn't know where I was…'

'There are only so many studios for Australian writers on the Right Bank – which, by the way, historically speaking, is the wrong bank – and isn't it about time you said, "Gee, what a lovely surprise and I'm so glad to see you"?'

There were no *Olympia* T-shirts or coffee mugs. There were, however, on sale for the discerning buyer, facsimiles of the choker necklace. Kate handed over her bankcard, wincing slightly. She saw nothing she could buy for Phillip. He would sneer at this stuff, call it kitsch. While she flicked through a rack of reproductions, Kate checked out the terminally chic young women behind the cash registers and absorbed a babble of languages.

She had almost given up hope when she found the Monet poster. It was a seascape but unlike the ones she had seen hanging on the walls that afternoon; they had been drenched in luminous cascades of pastel light and patrolled by women carrying parasols. This one was wild, undomesticated, with a sky which was a grey afterthought above a high horizon. Dark blue-green water snagged and eddied around black rocks; you could feel the primal suck of the ocean, measure the slippery height of stone. It reminded Kate of the place she had left, of the cold unforgiving water which cradled the bones of so many nineteenth-century ships and their human cargo, en route to the New World. She grabbed it up and paid, just as a loudspeaker informed her that the gallery would close in fifteen minutes.

A revived Venice waited outside the shop. She took a small hand mirror from her purse as Kate presented the choker and fastened it. 'Hey, it's raunchy.'

'Absolutely. You'd be my choice any time. Do you want to take a taxi back?'

'No, let's walk.'

They left the gallery and meandered along the Seine, past the metal booths set into the embankment selling postcards and paintings. A North African vendor tried to entice them with watercolours of Montmartre. Venice haggled. He shouted. Neither gave ground and in the end she bought nothing. Kate felt momentary sympathy for him, consigned no doubt to an outer suburb of the City of Light where he and his kind, beset by high unemployment and inadequate housing, periodically rioted and were told to eat cake.

Commuters rushed towards the Metro, thinner and better dressed than in her own country but with the same frantic light of escape in their eyes.

She and Venice crossed the river. They passed a cluster of lifestyle shops.

'Oh, let's just stop here for a moment…'

Kate's mobile rang.

'It's Phillip. I'm at Charles de Gaulle. What's going on?'

Kate breathed deeply, the way she had been taught years ago in a yoga class at the Ananda Marga ashram in North Fitzroy. Her text had said, urgent. come asap. Through plate glass, Venice fluttered and hovered like a manic butterfly.

'Your mother's here…'

'I don't want to see her.'

'She's sick, Phil.' All Kate knew about him warned her not to plead. 'The old crab's come crawling back.'

For several seconds all she heard was a tinny muzak thread of 'The Girl From Ipanema'. It faded, surged then faded. Phillip must be standing near a lift.

'How bad is it?'

'Pretty bad. She was having chemo, then they let her out and now she's here. She needs to see you, mate.'

'This may sound like a stupid question, Kate, but why didn't she phone?'

'You know what she's like, Phil. She's embarrassed about her behaviour. She's probably ashamed but can't admit it. But she needs to see you.'

There was a tangle of footsteps and voices. The lift had moved on to 'Do You Know the Way to San Jose?' Kate heard a thump, perhaps the sound of a travel bag hitting the floor, then the connection broke.

Venice strolled towards her, swinging three stylish carry bags by their corded handles.

Kate took her arm, felt the bone jut beneath flimsy flesh. 'He's on his way.'

Phillip, from the back seat of a taxi, watched the outer suburbs of Paris float by with the detachment of someone who had entered the far reaches of fatigue. The festival in Prague had gone on for three days and he had hardly slept. After his own gig, he had been too wired to settle: he and Meaghan had stayed up, talking and drinking with Liam and Stewie, the two guys he had hired to play with him, until dawn touched the twisting streets of the medieval city. He had seen Meaghan off to London, thinking he would join her in a couple of days, then a friendly Dutchman had sold him some speed.

Europe wasn't new to him. He had been here five years before, after Mira had told him their relationship was grotesque and had moved to Sydney, but this time he wasn't a homesick backpacker, scribbling songs. There had been a lot to listen to at the festival; there had also been plenty of chances to pick up and he had been tempted, very, but that was all behind him now.

He gazed out the window, at the faces coming towards him on the street. Cruelty, loneliness, some blank as glass, one which was radiant as an opening flower: the same old human animal, wherever you went. Phillip shifted on the seat; the girl's face had momentarily alerted his cock. He missed Meaghan but he would be with her in a few days, sitting while he listened to her banter with Anne, who must have looked just like her daughter thirty years ago, or having a whisky with Douglas while they put the world to rights.

Phillip didn't believe the old adage 'All happy families are alike but every unhappy family is different.' Happiness had its own subtleties, its own gradations. Unhappiness seemed by contrast monochrome and unrelenting: addiction, loneliness, despair. Perhaps it was just the fascination of the unfamiliar. Every time he turned into the tree-lined driveway leading to the seventeenth-century house where Meaghan had grown up, he felt the anticipation of a tourist entering a strange land.

'Thanks, mate.' Phillip winced when he saw the fare. However, the bloke had saved him a long inconvenient bus ride. He tipped generously, lifted out his bag and guitar then scanned the building, which looked like an Eastern European apartment block. He had heard about this place, which was actually a honeycomb of studios administered by the French government, but available to artists worldwide. Various Australian academic and arts organisations had leases here; if you were a writer, artist or musician and your work was deemed sufficiently worthy, you could use a studio for a while. Phillip couldn't see the point. Just looking at all that concentrated earnest endeavour made him claustrophobic.

He phoned Kate for directions, knowing he'd never negotiate this warren, and took some stairs as dusk came down and the glimmer of street lights illuminated the Seine. Blurry figures moved along the street, intensifying the melancholy which had hovered since his arrival at the airport. For a moment, he considered turning round. The French could be snotty sometimes but they were always curious about culture. He could make some money busking, take the Chunnel…

He heard Kate's voice. He knocked on the studio door.

When Kate hugged him, she felt small, like a child seeking refuge. Phillip had thickened in the waist and shoulders since he had left Australia three months ago. He wore a dark blue jumper like an old-fashioned fisherman's jersey, boots designed for mountain climbers and a heavy circlet of silver in one ear. She smelt sweat and soap and the oil from his shaggy black hair.

'You got here.'

'Looks like it.' He put down his luggage just inside.

Chaos and melodrama so often attended his mother that he was not surprised to see her stretched out on the sofa like a consumptive heroine in a nineteenth-century opera; however, instead of the traditional bloodstained handkerchief, she held a joint. She looked thin but cheerful, with her hair upswept in a glossy pile and her beautiful gold-flecked eyes glowing. Two cream candles impaled on black wrought-iron holders burned on the coffee table before her, giving off a pleasant vanilla scent almost obscured by the reek of hashish, and pale yellow wine pooled in goblets of translucent bluish-green glass.

After she had been given the all-clear the first time, Venice had once again taken up alcohol and cannabis, the old vices of her youth, abandoned when she detoxed from smack. 'I've tried living a pure life. It didn't do any good. If I'm going to go, then I might as well go pleasurably.'

Next to the sofa was a folding canvas chair and on it sat a thin, elegantly dressed woman Phillip had never seen before, her dark magenta lips compressed into a line of mingled tension and disdain.

'Baby!' Venice put down the joint and held out her hands, like a queen welcoming a subject. 'How's my handsome rock god?'

'Hello, Mum.' He stooped and kissed her on the cheek then drew back and held out his hand to the stranger.

'Phillip.'

'Françoise.'

'Françoise dropped in to have a drink with me…us.' Kate stood at the fridge with a second bottle in her hand and looked at him enquiringly.

Phillip shook his head. 'Scotch if you've got it, otherwise coffee.' He directed his attention to Françoise.

After she had separated from Anita, Kate had proclaimed an aggressive celibacy for some time. However, when her grant application had been approved, she had joined an internet dating service and made contact with a number of Parisiennes. Which one was this?

Françoise was the restaurateur. Phillip remembered Kate's hopes for 'great sex followed by great food'. He wished her luck but doubted it would happen. Françoise looked as though she might soil her dark magenta nails for diplomats, stockbrokers and minor aristocrats but not for some scruffy bohemian Aussie. And what did she make of Venice, silent and unattended, sucking on the joint so hard that it glowed red as an angry eye? His mother wore a black lace dress with a low neckline, swirling skirt and tight sleeves which ended in flounces. Around her neck was a piece of black ribbon from which hung a single teardrop, obviously imitation, pearl. It looked tacky, the kind of thing a girl on the game in Darlo would wear.

He listened as Françoise explained in heavily accented but fluent English, that her food was traditional but blended, freshened and enhanced by cuisines from France's erstwhile colonies. 'The best from many cultures.'

'So laudable, Françoise,' Venice murmured. 'Really, you're a veritable postmodern Margaret Fulton.'

Françoise, ignorant of the reference but aware that she was being mocked, drew her black brows together. 'Please, who is this person?'

'She's an icon, Françoise, a culinary guru from our large and backward land across the sea.'

'Françoise probably doesn't need to know who Margaret Fulton is.' Kate advanced from the tiny kitchen, Scotch in one hand, plate of biscuits and cheese in the other.

Phillip thought that she looked a bit panicky: she must be quite interested in this woman.

Venice pouted. 'The passionfruit sponge, the pavlova, these things do have a fascination for the uninitiated.' She turned abruptly to Phillip, holding out the joint. 'How's your girlfriend?'

Phillip inhaled, feeling the dense piney resin of hash expand inside his head. 'She has a name, Mum.'

'Oh, sorry. How's *Meaghan*?'

'She's good. She's with her parents in Kent at the moment.'

'I've heard it's lovely there.' Kate poured wine into glasses. 'The countryside's meant to be quintessentially English.'

'Oh, stop being such a fucking hostess!' Venice flicked ash in the direction of the metal dish on the table but most of it landed in a scrumbly grey pile on the floor.

Françoise shook her head, covered her glass with one hand and rose. 'I do have another engagement this evening.'

'Leaving so soon, Françoise?' murmured Venice. 'Sad.' She turned to Phillip again. 'Françoise was telling us that she has a very interesting sideline. She breeds small dogs, Pomeranians, I believe. I suggested that she should use them in the restaurant when she's preparing her Indo-Chinese dishes.'

Françoise contemplated her for a moment. 'I believe dog meat is not so bad to eat. In 1943, in the middle of the Occupation, my own grandparents ate dog, in order to have meat on the table. Indeed, Parisians have eaten dog – and rat – in other times, such as the Franco-Prussian War, when Paris was besieged. However,' she looked down at her flawless nails, 'I understand that these things do not 'appen in your country.'

Phillip wondered if Françoise carried a stiletto in her handbag. He glanced across at Kate, who was also on her feet, and almost laughed. Yep, definitely smitten.

Françoise picked up her handbag, extracted a Metro ticket, and clicked shut the interlocked-C clasp. 'I have been in your country,' she said by way of farewell. 'I found Uluru a most fascinating place. I have a small but lovely dot painting from there.'

Phillip measured the distance between his chair and the black case on the floor. Kate called him a twenty-first century troubadour; perhaps it was time to prove it. It would take three seconds to cross the space, collect his guitar and go. He looked across at Venice, who smiled her smoky odalisque's smile but said nothing. A small part of him felt sorry for her but mostly he was just bored. And he wanted to sleep, so badly, feel the earth slide away from him and bury this mess. He waited, his hands on his knees and his inner eye fixed on Meaghan's blonde-red hair, until Kate returned.

'I hope you're pleased with yourself.'

Venice waved a languid hand. 'The woman was a pompous prat. You're better off without her. It's time to eat. Do they have Hungry Jacks in Paris?'

Kate ignored her and examined Phillip. 'You look stuffed.'

'I am. I'm rooted, actually.' He laughed. 'They got their money's worth in Prague, I reckon.'

'You give a lot.'

'That's the point, isn't it?'

'I've got something for you. When I saw it, it reminded me of your song.' She was referring to his minor commercial success, the title song of his first CD, which he had written when he was last here.

Phillip spread out the scroll of paper and smiled. 'It's like home.'

'Sea pictures are in my mind,' she sang softly. 'The title's in French. I don't know what it means.'

'It's called *The Rocks at Belle-Ile, The Wild Coast.* It's a place where Monet stayed in eighteen…something or other,' Venice said suddenly. 'He made a number of paintings there. You can see the particular influence of Japanese prints…' Her finger traced the horizon line through air. 'Monet chose the greens and blues and purples then slashed them together to create an intense atmospheric vibration. Look at the brushwork, it's not like his earlier paintings. He doesn't dab. And yet there's something wistful there, I think, something almost gentle, if you look at the outcrops eternally attempting to encircle the little island.' She fell back onto the sofa and closed her eyes.

Phillip rolled up the poster. 'Thanks, Kate.' He glanced at the depleted plate of snacks. 'Let's get dinner.'

Kate didn't reply. It was easy to forget, when you looked at Venice, turned into a scrawny caricature by addiction, disappointment and illness, that there was still an intelligence at work which gleamed like a lost original through impasto layers of dross. It was Venice who had brought her here, really; Venice had been the one, years ago, who kept urging her to write. Kate said, quite gently, 'Thanks for explaining that, Rosie.'

'You're welcome.' Venice waved an airy hand then sat up. 'I'm starving.'

They sent out for pizza and while they waited she retired to re-pin her hair and add a pair of *cloisonné* earrings. She looked quite lovely, basking in candlelight, her eyes the same colour but with a deeper sparkle than the glass holding the wine. She set out to be charming, pressing Phillip for details of his time at the festival and wanting to know about his next project. Kate saw that he was courteous but unmoved: he had not forgotten the way Venice had behaved to Meaghan on her first, and only, visit to Australia.

Phillip hadn't given Kate all the details, just a sketch. 'She kept needling Meaghan, trying to put her down for being a mere commercial artist who designed CD covers. As though she has any claim to success.'

Meaghan, Kate had heard, had behaved with admirable restraint but then, her mother was an Anglican priest and her father a retired Marxist professor of economics: from her earliest years she had learned to steer a calm passage through rocky shoals. She hadn't responded to Venice's taunts, had asked politely whether she could view Venice's paintings, only to be told that Venice had made a big fire and burnt them all when she had been given her first diagnosis three years before.

'Since then I haven't bothered with art,' she told Meaghan, in a tone which indicated that it was, somehow, her fault.

Kate ungummed strands of mozzarella from cardboard and remembered something Phillip had once said. 'Mum was born out of her time. If she'd lived in an earlier age, she would have been a great courtesan, playing the lute and reciting poetry from a pile of satin cushions. Or, if she'd lived in the pagan era, she would have been a temple priestess, initiating young girls into the rites of the goddess.'

For some women, emancipation was not all it was cracked up to be. The old callings, which fused creativity and sex, were gone. Talents which might have formed a vocation became mere neurotic runoff, a malicious energy which delighted in fomenting squabbles and causing trouble.

Kate watched Phillip and Venice and didn't try to paste the cracks of fissured history. The situation was not hers and anyway, by the time Venice had retrieved the chocolate mousse from the fridge, Phillip was asleep.

'I'll make the sofa up for him.'

'Then where will I sleep?'

'You can bunk in with me.'

A search of a hitherto unexplored cupboard yielded sheets which were an unattractive dark beige but, thankfully, cotton. Memories of a six-year-old Phillip vehemently eschewing flannelette pyjamas printed with teddy bears, which she had bought on special at K-Mart, made Kate smile as she threw on the pillows.

'Wakey, wakey, mate.' She heaved him, grunting and stumbling, onto the sofa bed, took off his boots, twitched up the doona and left him to sleep fully clothed.

'Nightcap?' Venice held up a bottle of Dubonnet and two liqueur glasses.

'Why not?' Kate threw herself onto the bed behind the partition which looked as though it was made from plywood but to which the French probably gave a grander name. They clinked glasses then Kate switched off the Jacques Brel tape Venice had pushed into the player. 'You might think he's appropriate but I can't stand the guy.'

'He's a genius.'

'He's a moaner.'

Kate picked up Phillip's first CD. 'Sea pictures are in my mind, marbled waters, swirling skies…' They sat quietly, listening while he moved on to 'The Convincing Ground', which commemorated a group of Aborigines killed in a dispute with early European coastal visitors over a whale. There was a song of loss about a woman who had gone away for good. Did Anita ever play this song and think of her, Kate wondered. Probably not, or, if she did, it would be with relief.

'I wasn't too much, was I?' Venice asked suddenly. 'I wasn't over the top with him?'

'No, Rosie, you were fine.'

'I didn't want to scare him off.'

'You didn't.' Kate reached over and took her hand. 'He'd hardly be staying here if you had.'

'I've been stupid.'

'We all are, sometimes.'

'Why do we keep being stupid?'

Why indeed, Kate wondered. Stupidity was usually another name for fear or greed or anger. Most people would say she had been stupid, living three years with someone for whom she had, most of the time, felt no more than moderate affection, while the relationship hollowed out, inexorably, from the inside.

She put down the glass, saw the dregs congeal stockily at the base. 'I don't know.'

'I sometimes think I'm possessed by an evil spirit,' Venice laughed. 'But I know it's just my own insecurity.'

'Yes.' Kate reached over and stroked the glossy hair.

Venice frowned. Kate withdrew her hand.

'It's all right,' said Venice. 'I don't mind. It's just that this damn wig gets itchy sometimes.' She gave a sudden tug and the hair came away, revealing a dull, rust-coloured stubble underneath.

Seen like this, Venice's face was pale and denuded upon the freckled stalk of her neck. She placed the wig on one corner of the bedhead and patted it, as though praising an obedient animal. 'Don't worry,' she said. 'That's it. I left the merkin at home.'

Kate laughed. Venice had always been able to make her laugh. 'Come here, you ratbag.' She hummed a few bars of 'Bald-Headed Woman', an old blues Phillip used to play before he started using his own songs, and they both cracked up.

Kate undid the long row of buttons down the front of Venice's dress and unhooked the black bra. She pulled off her own shirt and jeans. 'Do you want me to turn the lamp off?'

'No, leave it on.' Venice lay outstretched, her thin pale fingers clasped behind her back.

A long horizontal scar bisected the site of her left breast. The scar was rutted and pitted like an old country road in summer but down its length, like jewels strewn along a rocky path, were tiny flattened ornaments of turquoise and gold. Kate put her finger on one of them, with the circumspection of someone investigating a land mine.

'I did think about getting a tattoo done,' Venice told her. 'But they're passé, really. Everyone has them now.'

Kate laughed again. It was typical that Venice would turn pain into beauty in this way; in the end, wasn't that all anyone could do? Kate ran her hand over the scar and down the length of Venice. She praised the valour of Venice with her lips and hands and tongue. Kate gathered Venice and all her pulsing dark energy, in her arms and Venice turned towards her with a clear warrior's gaze, her sea-green eyes fierce as a combative angel's. She wrestled Kate, with a fury which made them moan and cry but Kate held her, she stroked some of the deadly anger from Venice, until they rested in the river's blue light and heard the bells chime from distant Notre-Dame cathedral.

Phillip, dreaming of white sand and white horses, of spindly-legged foals running on the uplands, turned in his sleep but did not wake.

In the morning, he surfaced like a swimmer breaking the skin of a clean pool of water then washed, dressed and went out into the street.

A slender woman of a certain age sat at a café table and he was reminded briefly of someone he had once loved but who had not loved him. The woman at the café, with her smooth pale hair, her clothes of contrasting white and cream, her several broad silver rings and the burnished band which clasped one wrist, resembled Mira physically but it was more than that. She would be fastidious, like Mira, and guard her privacy fiercely.

Mira hadn't wanted to be seen in public with him, was afraid people would laugh at her. 'I'm not just old enough to be your mother, I'm old enough to be your grandmother.' For her, there had been no women's magazine cachet in having a toy boy. When she had used the word grotesque, Phillip had wanted to hit her but now he wished her well, although he doubted that she would ever be really happy.

Still, it had grown him up, that relationship; as he drew opposite the woman, sitting with her coffee over *Le Monde*, he gave her an admiring smile, which she returned with an amused ironic nod.

He was whistling an old Powderfinger song when he returned to the studio. Kate heard him and glanced across at Venice, who slept on her back, limp as a child's discarded rag doll. Kate shivered suddenly, pulled on a robe and went out as he placed a grease-stained paper bag down on the table.

'Sleep well?'

'I had a beaut sleep.' He held up the bag. 'Breakfast?'

They spread the croissants with butter and strawberry jam. There really was nothing like it, Kate thought, the saltiness of the butter mingling with the sugary jam, then washed down with good strong coffee. Phillip would have preferred sausages and bacon, she knew that, but he seemed happy to do as the Romans did. The dark thumb prints of fatigue beneath his eyes had disappeared but Kate saw the tension which corded his shoulders and threaded his sinews. She knew nothing about this woman he was involved with; he had emailed a photo of them clowning about on a pier at some seaside resort in Cornwall but what did a photo really prove? It showed a smiling rosy-cheeked blonde, who was not much older than a girl, someone Kate could imagine playing hockey. Would she be able to leave Phillip alone when she should and know enough not to pull him off course?

Kate split her second croissant inexpertly. 'You and Meaghan,' she began cautiously. 'Things are still good?'

'Yeah, we're good.' He reached for the jam. 'She's pregnant, actually.'

'Phil! Oh! Phil!' All the standard banalities of congratulation passed through Kate's mind. 'Well, you kept that pretty quiet.'

'I didn't want Mum to know. I still don't, okay? We'll tell her when we're ready. Anyway, we've only just found out.' He grinned at her across a table littered with pastry flakes. 'Prepare yourself to be a person of changed status, Granny.'

'Well…' That explained why he was under strain, although he seemed pleased enough. 'Well, I think that's great, Phil. Don't leave it too long to tell your mother. It might…' Kate stopped.

'…give her a whole new lease of life?' But he said it gently, almost compassionately, then grinned again. 'Knowing Mum, she'll start making up a Goth layette. Knit the kid black booties.'

'Or present you with a studded-leather bassinet,' Kate laughed.

'What are you two so happy about, this early in the morning?' Venice had wrapped a white and green nylon robe around herself. She faced them in her stubble and a pair of small, gold-framed glasses which gave her an earnest Nietzschean look as she lit the first cigarette of the day.

'Oh, take that outside,' Kate protested.

Venice scowled, muttered under her breath, shuffled to the door and slammed it behind her.

'What do you think has caused her to come out of remission?' Phillip placed the remaining croissants in the microwave.

'Who knows? Her cells are no good, that's all.'

Kate spoke dispassionately, with an undertone of weariness and Phillip noticed new lines engraved beneath her eyes.

Kate's early life was prehistory to him: he knew that she had been orphaned early, that her violent alcoholic father had left home when she was ten, 'Which was a good thing because it meant that Mum could enjoy her martyrdom alone.' There were three sisters and a brother, all still in Queensland. He had met the brother once, a blustering, big-bellied oaf who discouraged any thoughts of moving to that northern paradise. Phillip thought that this man had hurt Kate, had probably abused her, but he couldn't be sure. She had hit the road when she was sixteen with her first lover, a burly, freckle-faced Scot who had looked after her in return for sex. Once Phillip had asked Kate if she felt exploited by this and she had laughed. 'If it hadn't been for Big Mac, I'd have ended up in Winlaten, along with all the other lost little girls society didn't know what to do with. No, she saved me. She taught me about kindness.' Still, kindness had its limitations.

Phillip picked up the smeared plates and inky mugs and carried them to the sink. 'How long is Venice going to be here?'

'She said a week, so just a few more days.'

'Don't let her derail you. Not now.' He ran water and sloshed in detergent that the packet proudly proclaimed was *verte*. 'You know what she's like. Venice has an elastic sense of time. A few days may grow.'

'I can't kick her out, not now...'

He turned around and regarded her steadily. 'You've got to do your work, Kate.'

'Well, how do you advise I get rid of her?'

He stared out the tiny window. It had turned into a gritty sultry day. In the distance, a light pall of smog covered the outer suburbs. He heard the studio door shut.

'Is there breakfast?' Venice yawned.

Kate indicated the microwave.

Venice yawned again and stretched, so that one side of the robe billowed like a sail unfurled in a high wind. 'I'll shower first.' She stopped as she pushed open the door to the minuscule bathroom. 'What shall we do today? Perhaps we could go for a picnic in the Tuilleries. You remember that film, with Jane Fonda and Vanessa Redgrave? That funny little Austrian man approaches the Lillian Hellman character and says, "Shall we walk in the Tuilleries?" I've always wanted to walk in the Tuilleries.'

They heard her turn the water on.

Phillip threw cutlery into the drainer, dried his hands then turned around and asked, in a thick Viennese accent, 'And how vould you characterise your relationship mit Venice?'

Kate spread her hands. 'Love, guilt, dependency. The usual toxic female mix.'

'It doesn't seem to me that you've got much to be guilty about.'

Kate said nothing for a while. 'There was one night…this was just after you were taken into care… Venice was out of it, she was really out of it. I'd gone back on the dole…it was the middle of fucking winter. I looked at her and thought, "I don't want to be here any more. I don't want to do this any more." And I left her there. I didn't care. I left her to die. I hoped she would.'

The water stopped. Then it started again. Kate remembered that Venice often prolonged her shower, would stand under the spray for half an hour if you let her.

'But she didn't. She didn't die.'

'No, she lived.'

'That was then, Kate. This is now. Get over it.'

'Oh, listen to you, Doktor.'

The water stopped again. They chatted about nothing much.

After a few minutes, Venice emerged, head swathed in a towel. 'Well, the day is a blank page. What shall we write?'

'Let's go for that picnic, Mum.'

'You want to, baby?'

'Yeah, just the two of us, though. Kate has to work.'

'Oh, nice!' Venice smiled like a child let out of school for an unexpected excursion. 'We'll go to the Tuilleries?'

'Absolutely.'

'Oh!' Venice gave a little skip. 'We'll do some shopping, buy lots of nice things to eat and drink champagne.'

'Whatever you want, Mum.'

'Oh!' She gave another little skip on her way to the bedroom.

'Don't tire her out, Phil.'

'I'll be careful. The Tuilleries does sound like a sedate sort of place.'

It sounded bloody awful actually, full of trees clipped to within a centimetre of their lives and flower beds laid out in unrelenting oblongs and surrounded by raked gravel. The French seemed to hold a collective grudge against nature, given the way they shaped and pared her every chance they got.

Phillip unrolled the poster and looked at the roiling water. It must have been a challenge for Monet, trying to set down the salt-stained air and the fortress of rock but that was what you did: you went to new places. If you stood still, you stagnated and that was the end.

Venice came out of the bedroom dressed for the street, wearing a strapless black cotton sun dress and very high-heeled backless sandals. Her hair was piled on top of her head *à la* the young Audrey Hepburn. 'Well, let's go on this groovy picnic.'

'Breakfast first, Mum.' He pointed to the microwave. 'We'll come back this evening so that you can pack.'

'Oh.' Venice looked confused. 'We're going somewhere?'

'Somewhere else, Mum. We'll take a hotel for a few days, then we'll see. Perhaps I'll come back to Australia with you.'

Venice extracted her croissants. She gave him a brilliant smile. 'All right, baby. But let's not waste time. I'll leave these for later.' She turned to Kate. 'Looks like I'm out of here.'

'Yes.'

They looked at each other then at the same time looked away.

'The studio's small,' said Venice, 'and Phil needs a holiday.'

'He does.'

'We'll be back this evening. We'll get our things then.'

'Yes.'

'Thanks for putting up with me.'

'That's all right.' Kate realised she sounded grudging and ungracious. 'It's been wonderful to see you.'

'Oh, wonder-ful!' mocked Venice. She kissed Kate on the cheek. 'Work hard. We'll have a glass of champagne for you.'

Kate stood at the window, watching them recede and knew that she had reaped an unexpected reward. She felt humble then annoyed with herself for feeling humble. You put in the hard yards with a kid, did your best; weren't you entitled to expect something in return? No: it wasn't an investment plan with a guaranteed dividend. Kate watched Venice smile and turn her face up like a young girl and saw the way she tottered in those impossible sandals. She felt a quick sympathy although she knew it was superfluous; Venice wasn't feeling sorry for herself and that was the main thing.

All around her, the great city opened up for the day, laying out its history and treasures, its topiary and pavement art, for all those who cared to see. It watched Venice enjoying the company of a man who was possibly her son, possibly a younger lover, and was pleased for her. Kate smiled. She raised her hand just as her phone rang.

Phillip, waiting to cross the street, glanced behind and saw her, features already indistinct, her body a dark and solid oblong lifting its gallant fleshy star. He returned her salute even though his thoughts left her and crossed that aisle of choppy water to Meaghan and the unplanned creature now anchored determinedly within. If you were lucky, your parents nurtured you, loved you, brought you to a certain point of adult safety which enabled you to set out on your own. Inevitably, then, you began protecting them from the consequences of that journey.

Kate was entitled to her work. He could not burden her with his worries about money, about Meaghan, about the psychological machinations he would enter into with her parents who had offered to help out their daughter and her erratically earning partner. Phillip didn't want their help, he wanted to paddle his own canoe, but knew that it was a frail and leaky vessel. He might have to take a day job, give up music, at least for a while, or keep it as a hobby and suffer the slow erosion of spirit he had witnessed in others who did this. There was no easy way: England made him feel like a cuckoo, an alien in a too-small nest, but when he had suggested to Meaghan that they live in his home town, a place knitted into his blood and bone, she had asked whether there was a bookshop there and he had had to say, 'No. But there's three in the big place, which is only forty-five minutes away.'

He couldn't blame her for being apprehensive. He remembered how he had felt, coming to live there at sixteen, although it had been different for him. The seedlings he had helped plant all those years ago now clothed the hill as saplings, their whippy bodies still vulnerable to fire and storm but hanging on tenaciously. If Meaghan needed different soil for their child, then he would give up that storm-tossed strip of coast with its winds that howled up from the Antarctic and its purplish-indigo swells, on which a boat sat as precariously as a balsa raft, just to make her happy.

The lights changed. The traffic thinned for a heartbeat. As she stepped off the pavement, Venice let out a small exclamation. He had almost forgotten her, was dragged back to this place of palaces and bloodstained cobblestones and the smooth river which froze the bodies of suicides in winter.

'Are you all right, Mum?' He leaned over, concerned that this was a cellular skirmish which presaged a major battle.

'It's okay, baby. I've turned my ankle. It's these stupid shoes.'

He shouldered her weight while she massaged the afflicted joint and disdained any idea of resting.

'I'm quite all right but thank you for assisting poor crippled old me.'

'No worries, Mum,' he said quietly, calculating that Meaghan should be up and about by now. They would talk together soon. He waited until his mother was ready to move off. 'Come on, let's get going.'

After the call finished, Kate went into the bedroom and gathered up clothes. Her own were flung over a chair but Venice had strewn hers all over the floor. Kate made a few non-committal piles, tidying without intrusion. She found the choker lurking beneath the black lace dress and carried it into the kitchen, where she filled the kettle in order to review the conversation which had been conducted against a symphonic backdrop of saucepans. Kate had thought Françoise's declared intention to phone, made the previous evening, mere politesse but here she was, supervising an ensemble of chefs while waiting to extend her knowledge of Australian literature.

'The other night, at dinner, I asked you about your novel and all you would say is, "It has nothing to do with Jacques Lacan".'

'That's true,' said Kate. 'There is a distinct lack of Jacques Lacan.'

'So, what is it about?'

'Oh, the usual things: Love, Death, Art, Representation.'

'What, there is no madness?'

'No,' said Kate. 'Well…a *soupçon*. Would you like there to be madness?'

'No,' replied Françoise. 'Order, civility, these are good things.'

'Yes,' said Kate.

There was a clash of metal in the background.

Françoise fired off rapid instructions in French. '*Excusez-moi.* The usual minor catastrophe. Your friend is still with you?'

'Yes. No. She's leaving tonight.'

'Ah, she is not well, I think.'

'No.'

'That is sad.'

'Yes.'

It is likely she will die. But she would not tarnish Françoise's shining possibility with the words.

Françoise mentioned a restaurant that Kate had heard of, excessively expensive but with brilliant food. 'There is no dog on the menu and it is, as you say in your country, my shout.'

'I was hoping I might see your restaurant.'

Françoise laughed. 'Only if you promise to tell me all about Margaret Fulton.'

Kate sat at her desk, holding the choker. She saw that a tiny pit already scarred the teardrop pearl. Venice wouldn't look after it, would leave it lying around so that the jewel became scratched and the velvet robbed of plush. Eventually it would end up in a drawer with other bric-a-brac. Kate sniffed it cautiously; it gave off the odour of used and sweaty female flesh, flesh she had once known as well as her own and from which she had helped birth another living being. The flesh had its own history and its own memory, it sang across the gulf of years and pierced you with lost possibility: what could have been, what should have been. *Get over it.* Words, cold and sharp as a surgical blade: if only the past could be excised so neatly.

Kate flung the choker away as though it would contaminate her. She got up and moved restlessly around the studio, which for the first time seemed too small, then turned abruptly and swept all the books and papers off her desk. Then she sat down and let out the primal tearing sounds of a she-wolf. Tears and snot ran down her face. She cried until she was emptied out and there was a pile of scented French Kleenex on the desk. When she knew there was nothing left, she went into the bathroom, turned the tap on and let it run until she had rinsed off the residue of grief. She walked through the studio, disregarding its detritus and switched on the kettle.

As she dropped a spoonful of instant coffee into a mug, she hummed a fragment of Phillip's song. Before he was born, there had been a steamy summer's day when she and Venice, weary of the sticky streets and of each other, had driven out of the city, driven for hours with the wind rasping sweaty skin, until they reached a shallow strip of coast pitted with inlets and bays. They had trudged down to a small cove where crinkling pale green water swept dark moss and the shifting grit of shells. They stripped and swam and brought each other to orgasm beneath a grey sky overlaid with humid yellowish light.

Later they spread the picnic rug then realised they had nothing for it except a four-litre container of water and apples they had forgotten to take in from the previous day's trip to the market.

'Oh, well,' said Venice, daintily slicing, 'it does remove the agony from choice.'

The first thunder sent them scrambling for their clothes, orange skirt and jade shawl whipping against a cobalt sky as they raced for the cliff-top. Light-headed from hunger, they held hands in the refuge of the car and watched spindly lightning dance across the sea and it had not occurred to Kate that any of it was miraculous, that this was a day to remember, one which, if you reflected upon it later, you might have wished to go on and on.

9 781760 411237